4

P9-AOD-585

The Year
Roger
Wasn't Well

ALSO BY SARAH PAYNE STUART
Men in Trouble

The Year Roger Wasn't Well

A NOVEL

Sarah Payne Stuart

HarperCollins*Publishers*

All the characters in this novel are fictional, *especially* the main character.

HarperCollins books may be purchased for educational, business, or sales promotional use. For information please write: Special Markets Department, HarperCollins Publishers, Inc., 10 East 53rd Street, New York, NY 10022.

Designed by George J. McKeon

Library of Congress Cataloging-in-Publication Data
Stuart, Sarah Payne.
  The year Roger wasn't well : a novel / Sarah Payne Stuart.
—1st ed.
    p. cm.
  ISBN 0-06-017079-4
  1. Young women—Massachusetts—Boston—Fiction. 2. Marriage—Massachusetts—Boston—Fiction. 3. Boston (Mass.)—Fiction.
I. Title.
PS3569.T826Y43 1994
813'.54—dc20   93-38888

94 95 96 97 98 ❖/HC 10 9 8 7 6 5 4 3 2

To Donnie, and to Cissy

I would especially like to thank Sandy Frazier and Charlie Stuart.

Also for their expertise, I would like to thank Chip Benson, Liz Darhansoff, Alisa Dougless, Sheila Gillooly, Jeannie Jordan, Patty Marx, Deirdre McDonnell, Abigail Thomas, Priscilla Warner, and Judy Wolfberg.

Finally, for their wonderful editing, I would like to thank Robert Jones and Rick Kot.

The Year
Roger
Wasn't Well

1

A Short Career in Public Television

"I pray every night that you do not go to law school," her mother said, as Lizzie perused the help-wanted section upon her somewhat inglorious return to Westchester County the February of 1974. She hadn't a clue what she wanted to be. She'd spent four years at Harvard and never done a lick of work, due to social obligations. All she cared about was boys; she'd grown up amidst the fires of Women's Liberation and emerged unsinged. And yet now, as she lay, week after week, smoking cigarettes on her parents' living-room rug, she wondered if perhaps some application to the course material might have been desirable.

Every night her father would return from work to find her resting in approximately the same position he'd left her in. "What's new?" he would ask brightly, in the wild hope she would have an answer. At last, one day, for no apparent reason, she decided to go into "broadcasting." She discussed it solemnly with her parents, none of them admitting that into each mind had sprung the image of Mary Tyler Moore—single, at twenty-nine! and yet throwing that hat up into the air—instilling in all souls a sense of renewed calm. She wrote to all the W call letters in the Manhattan phone book, and in June, landed a job writing ads for the radio station in nearby Hartsdale, where all the guys were salesmen-types and married. She tried to be creative but pretty much all you were given to work with was the first line, "Zing into spring at D'Adamino's garden center . . . " and then you had to cram in about a hundred and fifty prices.

This lasted until September, when she took a day off from writing about the continental cuisine at Rudy's Beau Rivage to drive up to Boston to interview at WPRV, the city's public television station, where everyone was a liberal and had long hair. The idea had hit her one day soon after her parents—not that they cared about the *money*, but because it would teach her responsibility—decided to start charging her rent. As she turned off the Mass Pike onto Memorial Drive in Cambridge, the September sun was glistening in the dirty water of the Charles River, upon whose shores she'd jogged with Richard Townsend, been depressed with Tommy McGuire, and once, after she'd gotten in a car accident with a bunch of jetset preppies, gotten jostled, for a brief, shining moment, by young Joe Kennedy. She was back! She parked her Subaru in the parking lot of WPRV with the fullest of hearts. She knew that her life was just beginning, that soon she would fall in love and be happy forever and ever.

To some, it might just have been a job interview.

"All my *life* I've wanted to help the hearing impaired!" she burst out during the interview, the sudden affection she felt for a cameraman walking by in Ben Franklin glasses infusing this statement with a warmth that brought a tear to her interviewer's eye.

Lizzie sneaked another peek over her interviewer's head to the hallway beyond. There they were, droves of them, wandering the hallways in rumpled hair and blue workshirts, like little lost boys. Not since the March on Washington had she seen such a collection of her type! Waves of emotion swept over her. She nearly leaped from the chair in her enthusiasm for captioning the news for the deaf, being extra careful, however, not to dwell on the news angle. She hadn't been able to bring herself to so much as glance at the front page of a newspaper since the eighth grade. Not that she wasn't terribly liberal, once she figured out which side *was* liberal. Recently she'd dreamed she was captured by the Sandinistas and had had to stop the dream because she couldn't remember whether you were supposed to *like* the Sandinistas or *hate* the Sandinistas.

On and on went the interview in the glass cubicle in the WPRV Caption News Center, Lizzie explaining how much it would mean to her to do her little bit to help. She was nearly crying by the end, and it was all Ted—or was it Jed, this nice shy man in his forties, dressed incongruously in a 1950s suit—and she could do to keep from throwing each other into each other's arms, in their shared mission.

She felt a little bad about this an hour and a half later, when she accepted the job down the hall typing for "Stage Classics." She had liked Ted/Jed, and certainly, when she'd had a chance to think about it, it would have been nice helping others, but she simply didn't have the luxury of a choice. She had to take the typing job; the captioning job was at night, when there were fewer guys around.

*   *   *

The WPRV cafeteria was where all romance germi-
nated—the intense looks between couples discussing
racism or ginger root in low tones weighing the air with
a sexual promise you could cut with a knife. "I'm just
passionate about racism!" Josh Hay had announced one
lunchtime to Mimi something or other, the serious new
production assistant with the hourglass figure, banging
his fist upon the table. The only time Lizzie made an
impression, unfortunately, was on the day she put her
hard-boiled egg in the microwave to warm it up, and it
being her main course, pressed the button marked "dinner." It was amazing, really, how many particles one little
egg could explode into, sticking into every nook and
cranny of the place; it had almost made her believe in
atoms.

The egg incident took place at the beginning of her
second month at the station, on a breathtaking October
day when she had been trying to make an impression on
Chas, the director of "Stage Classics" with whom she
had been included in a working lunch. Why she had been
included, she did not know. Maybe she was supposed to
take notes, or maybe it was supposed to be educational,
or maybe it was to get her away from her desk, where
she would otherwise be doing damage. She couldn't type;
whenever she got near an electric typewriter, semicolons
would appear out of nowhere. "It; is; good;; to work;
ha;rd," she had pounded out at record speed on the typing test. She had been lucky PRV was so liberal; the per-
sonnel lady had just ripped up the typing test after the
third try. It wasn't supposed to matter if you could type
in public television; she was a Harvard girl, after all—
here was the one place in the world that characterization
triumphed over competence. But she was, it was discovered with astonishing speed up to the top level of the station, outstandingly bad.

What was so pathetic was how hard she tried, just as she had tried hard at all the other jobs she had ever had. Contrary to the teachings of her suburban youth, she had learned, it was *results*, not attitude, that mattered. Who would ever have guessed it? Growing up, back before her brothers' troubles, when her brother Harry was still the star and had been given the A minus in English, not because he wasn't doing A work but because he wasn't *trying* his hardest, her parents had ushered him solemnly into the living room and closed the double doors. "All that matters is that you do your best," she had been told over and over. But guess what—nobody cared that you tried your hardest, if still you were incompetent. What a betrayal to the concept of life in Concord, Massachusetts! Historic Concord! Where the street names recall Henry David Thoreau with a fondness quite absent during his lifetime (when he was regarded by the townspeople as little better than a hooligan), and every ten years the matrons play Meg, Jo, Beth, and Amy, with a somewhat mature sweetness, the husbands fleeing before intermission. Concord, where her mother had taken French on Tuesdays and drawing lessons on Fridays— year in and year out. Her mother, who hadn't an ounce of talent as an artist of charcoal trees, and knew it, but home she would come dutifully with some indiscernible third-grade smudge.

But now, it turned out, it was what you *did* that counted! Lizzie was twenty before this distressing detail about real life began to nudge its way into her vision, waitressing at Ye Olde Pie Shoppe in California, where she'd fled after dropping out of college after Harry's shock treatment. She was a miserable waitress, pea soup running down the front of her colonial garb, order forms crumbling to sticky wadded balls in her apron pocket. All she wanted in life, she was quick to realize, was a lunch break, and yet how hard it had been to land the job of telephone operator that came with two(!) coffee breaks. Over she had gone to the big windowless telephone company building every week on her day off and vainly filled out the application form. They didn't care she'd gotten into Harvard; they didn't care she scored 100 percent on the admissions test! Finally she'd stormed into Mr. Romanoff's office demanding to know why, after four applications, she'd been rejected again.

"Frankly, Miss Reade, you just don't look businesslike," he had said. So, to replace the faded maroon Indian print shirt and thong sandals, she had bought a Ban-lon dress that (only later she discovered) had bunny rabbits lurking amidst its flowered print, a nylon headband, and a pair of blue, fake leather shoes.

"Well, *that's* more like it!" Mr. Romanoff had beamed as Lizzie bustled off to get her picture I.D., "you will go far." And oh, she had been A plus right through the three-day training program. "Isaac Pearlman," the teacher had called out while twenty girls with beige hair flipped the corners of their phone books with the eraser tips of their pencils. But it was she who, in the pregnant pause, raised her hand and said in a calm, but compassionate voice, "I am sorry, I do not find that number listed." And then, after clapping her approval the teacher had explained how, for a certain low percentage of "perhaps my supervisor can assist you"s, you got a petal sticker for your headset, which in due time would become a colorful flower. "To show the world a job well done," the teacher said, at which point Lizzie couldn't help thinking that somebody'd better clue these people in that nobody could see them over the phone. But she had curbed her naturally sarcastic tongue (she knew sarcasm was the defense of the weak, but it was her only gift), graduated the course with high honors, and presto, she was on the board, which to her horror did not consist of comfy phones with receivers but headsets that beeped once before each call careened in. She'd fallen apart, swiveling madly between phone books, beseeching God, while out the corner of her eye she'd seen the other girls, who had once (the day before) seemed so lifeless, breezing along with smooth confidence. She had been fired before the week was out.

If WPRV had been real life, she supposed she might not have lasted through her first day, but then of course if WPRV had been real life she would have never been given the secretarial job in the first place, so in a way, it served them right. Her first day she had stayed till 9:00 P.M. glued to her typewriter, every muscle of her body tensed, striving to type a one-line internal memo from her boss to the general manager of the station, saying the screening of such-and-such show had been changed from September 22 to September 24. Her boss could have typed it in less than a minute, but instead her own smeared, unaligned memo was sent off in the first pickup the next morning. "Who in the *world* is responsible for this?" came out of the mouth of Jeremy Showalter, the fastidious general manager with the clacking heels and bow ties, whom her boss Marsha and sub-boss Sybil thought *so* handsome.

She was a lousy secretary, a mess really, with stray shoes sticking out of her desk drawers. But the theory was, of course, that her lowly job typing was just a stepping-stone to the thing she would do so well, that soon she would be whizzing ahead to becoming a producer. Her official title was "production secretary," but she'd been promised some work as "production *assistant*," whatever that was, which she was supposed to be eager to obtain. And so the associate producer, Sybil, who had once been Marsha's secretary—a fact that lingered heavily in the air between them still—had sat her down one Friday afternoon and explained all kinds of technical matters, involving the pressing of this button and that button and the calling up of technicians who worked in some subterranean quarter. With Job-like patience she had guided Lizzie through each procedure, waving her long red fingernails about and talking in a saccharine, gladder-to-be-condescending-to-than-be-condescended-to voice that sent a pleasant, mesmerizing chill down Lizzie's spine. She, production-secretary-now-production-assistant, at least for this exciting moment, had nodded wisely, not comprehending a single word, but gathering, finally, and to her rudely awakened horror, that the point of this soothing chat was that it was to be Lizzie, not Sybil, who would come to the station Saturday morning at 7:00 A.M. to perform this mysterious function.

She arrived on the designated morning at 6:30 on the dot, signed in with an efficient bustle and walked briskly, her size nine brown corduroy bell bottoms making a little rhythmic whirr as she strode down the corridor and into the editing room, with the quiet air of a woman who knew what she was about. For twenty-eight minutes she calmly awaited commands from below, viewing emotionlessly her adversaries the TV monitors and the other boxes and wires that evidently were to concern her. She picked up the phone at its first ring at 7:00 and listened with a somber air to the various instructions, taking copious but unintelligible notes. She had taken speedwriting two summers before with the sole but significant result that her borderline handwriting was now completely illegible. Then she'd hung up the phone, closed her eyes, and pressed what she hoped was an appropriate number of buttons.

She never knew the exact amount of money she had cost the station that day, but she had evidently made a point, for no one ever asked her to so much as lower the volume on a TV set again. On the down side, however, this little run-in with the machines had made it clear rather early on that here was yet one more thing, like being a good driver, that would have to be crossed off the lists of things she could possibly be good at.

But then, at last, after the first hopeless month on the job, there it was, like a gift from above, she found that she was a whiz at transcribing hours and hours of turgid interviews with academics about plays nobody would ever watch. In the transcript field a plethora of semicolons and mysterious foodlike imprints was overlooked in favor of speed. Indeed, reading the transcripts was so tedious that anything that deviated from the expected course was greeted with faint relief by the transcript readers, whose job it was to cut them down from five hours to ten minutes. The importance of these transcripts in the general scheme of things might be doubted. But no one who was in the know could deny that in the context of "Stage Classics—The Humanities in Drama," the transcripts had their place.

There was a great deal of hubbub around the station about "Stage Classics—The Humanities in Drama" (this zippy little title, which nobody understood, had been concocted by the staff, a gun to their heads by their chief funder, the National Endowment for the Humanities), and enormous grant money spent, and it was a few weeks before it dawned on Lizzie that in fact the show consisted of already-produced shows brought over from England. She'd been under the vague impression, based on the flurry of work always to be done at life-or-death speed, that some of these plays were to be produced in the United States. But no: WPRV's sole function was to produce short introductions to fill in the gap where the BBC commercials had been.

It seemed a simple enough proposition, she'd thought, with Marsha traveling first class over to London to view shows and bring them back. Rather a cushy job, really, and yet Marsha always seemed in the midst of some kind of nervous breakdown, due to severe overwork, dragging all sorts of equipment home with her every Friday, enlisting the help of various members of the (all male) PRV camera crew. Down the corridors she would scurry, papers rustling and earrings jangling, barking out commands to those in her wake—so overwhelmed by the burden of rebroadcasting shows, she felt forced to delegate even the most minor details of her personal life. "Maybe I should get Elizabeth to hem my pants," Marsha had said with a large cigarette-puffed sigh of exhaustion at the first production meeting, just as Lizzie had been sitting there trying to pretend she was a little important, what with the one male on the show, Chas the director, present. "Hem my pants!" to Lizzie who had broken two sewing machines in home economics during the year it took her to make the turquoise polished cotton A-line shift that didn't fit. Lizzie who couldn't sew a button on her coat without getting the pocket somehow involved. (And who cared what Marsha looked like, anyway, Lizzie had thought later, she was forty-eight! When Lizzie had read that on some form she was typing she had almost fallen off her chair. How could anyone be so old and still care about how her pants looked?) Fortunately, Marsha had settled for sending her downtown to Newbury Street to pick up her china, a venture that had only cost Lizzie (who might as well have been asked to drive to Siberia with her sense of direction) personally $14 in cab fare.

Sybil did not fare much better at the hands of Marsha, but Sondra could do no wrong. Sondra Venn was a senior researcher, but before she'd worked for Marsha, she'd worked for the very chic, high-budgeted show "Real World," whose staff had lunched on fine wine and Salade Niçoise at the Henry IV. As a result, although twenty years younger, Sondra was paid more than Marsha, who had taken the longer, more plebeian route. Sondra was six years older than Lizzie, turning twenty-nine the first week Lizzie was at the station. She was not technically pretty—there was something askew about her nose—but she was the sort that other girls thought beautiful because she was thin with perfectly fitting gabardine pants, and her purse was an expensive leather pocketbook and had never been, Lizzie was sure, a canvas pony express bag with an ink blotch growing insidiously in the corner. Her perfectly straight mahogany hair divided cleanly in the middle, swinging in shining sheaths from side to side as she glided about in neat, catlike movements. Sondra was married to Tye, who was independently wealthy, and always seemed to be at work on some article about electronics. "The great thing about my money," Tye had explained affably to Lizzie, "is there's not quite enough income to live on, so one has to *do* something."

Sondra was an agreeable, clever girl and very nice to Lizzie, and yet Lizzie could not help but think of her as Becky Sharp, with the slight bend to the nose that Thackeray gave his heroine in her otherwise fine-featured face. Still, Lizzie had always liked Becky Sharp, and thought that if Becky had been allowed the luck to marry well as Sondra had, she, too, would have been an agreeable girl.

Such was the bevy comprising the "Stage Classics" unit, attractivish women ranging from early twenties to late forties. Marsha, though the leader, lost her courage around Sondra, her lower jaw giving way to a jowl, her hair frazzling, her eyes smarting from her cigarettes, as Sondra (the only one who did not smoke in 1974) swiveled around in her chair, as perfectly eyelined at 6:00 P.M. as she had been at 10:00 A.M. Marsha worshipped her; Sybil, remodeling her impossible ranch house and trying to like her always-a-pencil-in-the-breast-pocket-computer-programmer husband, envied her; and Lizzie held on to her. Sondra was all she had, in that Sondra was the only one of the group that treated her with respect.

But the one who worshipped Sondra the most was Hills Todd, the man upon whom Lizzie's wild gaze alighted the morning she learned her days might be numbered.

2

Hills

Everyone was very idealistic and very caring at WPRV, a state of being that seemed to lead to a great many extramarital affairs, but it wasn't until January, after the doctor had examined her and gone white in the face, that Lizzie's romantic life was to get into swing. "Uh, there seems to be a little problem on the ovary here," the doctor had said in a startlingly casual voice, if you happened to be comparing it at that moment to his stricken expression. For an instant, sitting in that office with all the religious pictures scotch-taped to the walls, Lizzie thought, "Maybe I'm going to die." She was always imagining she was going to die; from time to time she'd envisioned herself wasting away in a purple silk gown, with everybody, particularly the people she was mad at at the moment, gathered about grieving vociferously. But now it struck her rather forcibly that getting everybody sad for her wasn't perhaps worth dying for.

As she drove back to the station, she decided to look on the bright side of the operation (which wasn't to happen for six weeks). When she'd had her tonsils out in

high school, after all, she'd managed to lose five pounds.
And how she'd loved being in the hospital, where everybody took care of you and padded about in soft shoes,
whispering so as not to disturb you, and you lay on that
hard, cool bed in the operating room with all the masked
nurses busy as beavers (you didn't even have to make the
token gesture of asking, "Is there anything I can do?"),
and then you tried to hold on as long as you could before
going to sleep after the shot because this, this surely was
heaven.

By the time she arrived back at the PRV cafeteria, she
was considerably perked up. And there, sitting by himself
in a little ray of sunlight, was Hills Todd.

Hills was very handsome, in an airedale sort of way,
with curly brown hair and deep brown eyes slitted in a
long, sharp face, creased with the weight of a myriad of
self-assumed responsibilities. He was a bachelor at thirty-
seven and, though dressed like a boy in blue workshirt
and corduroys, he viewed life sighingly as a man who
accepted that he was born privileged and felt an obliga-
tion to those privileges, whether it be taking the proper
care of the BMW sedan he was fortunate to own or ful-
filling his debt to society by taking on his current, hopelessly mismatched job as executive producer for a black
kids' show, "RIGHT ON!"

Poor, beautiful, sad-faced Hills Todd, the most eligi-
ble bachelor in Cambridge, was quietly trying to get
down his refined palate a tuna fish sandwich from the
machine, when this vision of teeny-bop in beige denim
miniskirt and purple gauzy—there is no other word for
it—tunic, plopped herself down across from him at the
table and said, "Hi, don't you just feel like going out and
spending a lot of money on a really good meal?"

It was a pure miracle that she'd hit upon this lucky
topic with Hills, who was fond of saying he preferred to

dine rather than eat. By really good meal, of course,
Lizzie had meant just about anything other than the
burnt frozen Italian green beans and cottage cheese sandwiches (her own invention) she supped on. She had happened on this riveting conversation-opener with the view
of eventually, but delicately, hinting to Hills that she
would like to go out and eat this meal with *him*.

But Hills was a harder nut to crack than some, and
their bright, sprightly conversation about restaurants and
food dragged on and on, until finally, finally, Hills said
something along the line of, why don't we try out such
and such a restaurant sometime? Like tomorrow! she
fairly yelled out in exasperation. Why not? said Hills,
and soon, heaving a little sigh, she returned to work.

She was whistling a happy tune until the next morning when she ran into Hills coming up the stairs, and
thought, judging by his dour expression, it's all off. This
upset her, even though at the same moment she was
noticing Hills wasn't looking so great. He was wearing
one of those tan, amorphic cashmere "casual" sweaters,
V-necked, that mothers give their grown-up sons in the
subconscious effort to keep women away from them, and
it made his skin look pasty and his body hint of flabbi-
ness around the tummy.

It seemed, she was informed solemnly, that Hills's
older brother had just gotten into some kind of financial
scrape, and Hills felt it would be "inappropriate" for
them to go out and have a fancy dinner that night. Not
because of the expense, he explained; it just wasn't to his
taste after his brother's profligacy. Certainly Lizzie's
immediate sympathy leaned toward the brother, who had
probably committed the sin of spending principal instead
of interest, and for a brief, wild instant, she thought of
mounting a defense for him in the hope of saving their
date. But it soon became apparent that what Hills really

had in mind was simply going to a less expensive restaurant. So that night, she drove her bashed-up little Subaru over to Hills's apartment off Brattle Street, where a few of his friends were gathering for cocktails.

Lining the walls of his long front hall was a gallery of pictures of Hills listening handsomely to John Dean, Henry Kissinger, and other political figures he had worked with on "Real World." The display seemed a bit ostentatious to Lizzie, but she was too young to let a little thing like personality affect her romantic proclivities. She sped by them, appearing breathlessly in the large, beautifully furnished living room, stifling the urge to crawl under the vast lemon-polished coffee table strewn with coasters (coasters!) and cocktail napkins.

She asked authoritatively for a gin and tonic (the only name of a cocktail that sprang to mind), rather to Hills's embarrassment, she was to learn later, when, unable to contain himself, he broke down at one of his friends' gourmet dinner parties and informed her that one didn't drink gin and tonics in the winter.

How relieved she had been to learn early on that Hills's friends called him "Sam"—how could you call someone "Hills" in bed? she'd been thinking to herself— but then Hills said he didn't think it quite right that *she* call him Sam, and so it was "Hills" she slept with after their tenth night out in a row. She had suggested the first night that it would be more fun if they waited, and Hills had found this so refreshing, he'd waited through nine more dates, embarking at last on the affair with a grim tenacity, as if she were the last duty of the day. After that, they'd spent every night together, except for that special time in the month when Hills thought she might be more comfortable in her slum apartment with the female rock drummer pounding away.

"Move in with us!" her brother Spencer and his girl-

friend, Boo, had said to her back in September. And so
Lizzie had driven up from Westchester and moved in
with Spencer and Boo, who promptly broke up the very
next day. And then it was, "I want you to stay because
you remind me of Spencer!" from Boo every morning as
she burst into a fresh downpour of tears, until after two
weeks it became "I think you should leave because you
remind me of Spencer!" also with a fresh downpour of
tears. And so she had packed up her backpack and moved
from the cozy apartment on Harvard Street to the seedy
apartment of the female drummer behind Central Square,
whom her other brother, Harry, had lived with the week
before his third breakdown—if you can be said to have
lived with someone without having slept a single wink.

Shelley was a white-blond, salacious-eyed woman
with a nasal twang whose sneering gaze bounced out at
you from the mirrored walls that lined the hallway of her
horrible apartment. "I'm supposed to be happy in eleven
days," she had honked in greeting, shaking a bottle of
pills, and then she had turned on the expensive stereo
system that allowed the listener to hear not one, but four
Shelleys singing slightly off key.

Lizzie should have been happy living with the female
drummer, because Shelley had put an ad in the *Phoenix*
for musicians for the band she was trying to form, and
every day, when Lizzie came home from work, there were
assembled the mangiest, most tangled-haired lot of characters sitting in a line from front door to refrigerator on
the dirty linoleum floor. Lizzie had a habit of falling for
depressed guys—she used to fall in love whenever she'd
watched her brothers play basketball at the local mental
hospital—but Shelley's recruits were too sorry even for
her. As she stepped over them on the way to her cell off
the kitchen, she felt as perky and clean-faced as Mary
Richards in a new pair of pantyhose.

At the beginning of their third week together, Hills presented Lizzie with the key to his apartment. "Don't abuse the privilege," he warned, dampening the romantic effect, and causing the key in her hand to feel suddenly warm from the hand of the last so honored. There was a great deal of drinking and dining out, which gave the relationship a kind of dashing-off excitement. But when she found herself sitting in a man's shirt across the dining-room table from Hills one Saturday morning, breaking up an egg in a porcelain eggcup and listening to him talk about the sadnesses in his life, she was strangely unmoved.

And yet by the third week of their courtship, they were proceeding inexorably, if not exactly merrily, along as if they were to be married any day—it was only a matter of setting the date. On they went, discussing the finances of *their* future like a couple married ten years. "I'll support us now, and then you'll support us in my old age," Hills said after she'd dredged up the worn idea of her going to law school. Then after their third visit in a month to her great-aunt Elizabeth and-uncle Win, who happened to be rich and childless, and who she generally saw once a year, tops, Hills had had a serious talk with her about "the things."

"Oh, it's all going to Harvard and the museums," she'd said, not as yet particularly caring. Hills had frowned and said, "I think you should let your aunt and uncle know how much you care about the furniture."

She supposed that matters were whirling along as if toward marriage, because marriage was the only vocabulary she allowed herself to use. All she had ever wanted was to get married; her mother and she had planned her wedding at each house the Wendell Mattress Company had moved them to. She couldn't imagine sleeping with anyone unless marriage was somewhere in the background as a possibility (although, she was finding as the years marched on she was able to fall in love rather more swiftly).

Since the second week of the relationship she had been dropping by her apartment only to pick up clothes, Hills's BMW running outside as she dashed by Shelley in her carpenter pants, a sardonic smile on her Gumby face. "You shouldn't be embarrassed about where you live," Hills had said. "We've all lived in garretts; I only just moved to my present apartment two years ago." One day she finally relented and brought him in (where a rock had been thrown through the living-room window the day before), leading him past the ceiling-to-floor mirrors in the hallway, past the overflowing ashtrays and toppled Chinese food cartons left over from the band rehearsal of the previous night, and into her tiny bedroom, a true *bed*room, for that was all the furniture it could hold. Hills stood on the gouged linoleum floor, next to the oak bed that had been found on the sidewalk on Harvard Street and was now fully set up, except that because Lizzie had never gotten around to getting bottom slats, the mattress, though within the bed frame, was settled on the floor, like a kitty litter box. And Hills Todd took in "Tarpit," made from a kit and featuring a prehistoric creature sinking into tar while above him a vulture watched from a tree; and next to this scene, "Cloret," the alligator ashtray she'd bought as a memento of the night she spent trying to sleep on the floor of the Miami airport. As Hills studied her "things," and Shelley (who never cooked) slammed pots and pans in the adjoining kitchen, Lizzie knew it had been a mistake, after all, bringing Hills there.

"You think I'm an old fart, don't you?" Hills said.

"No, no," she said, "no!"

*   *   *

She had barely glimpsed Shelley since the advent of Hills, but apparently her absence had not improved their relationship, for six days away from her operation, Shelley slouched into the kitchen where she was downing a quick cottage cheese sandwich for old times' sake, and indicated with a variety of snorts and honks that she wanted Lizzie to move out.

"And you can take your fucking cottage cheese with you!" Shelley concluded, and to illustrate her point, opened the refrigerator door and began flinging the Lite n' Lively containers around the room. It took a mere two days for Lizzie to locate, for a large fee, a wretched, insecure ground-floor apartment next to a defunct Mobil Station in Porter Square, at about twice the rent she had been paying.

"Good for you!" said Ms. Greenette, the social worker she'd been seeing at fifteen bucks a whack (a deal, until you looked at what you got) to discuss how she felt about her operation, before she gave Lizzie the dewy-eyed look that announced her launch into her favorite topic. "Might it be, Elizabeth," said Ms. Greenette softly, "that what you really want . . . is a baby?" Lizzie sighed and thought once again that Ms. Greenette, who was thirty-five, and in spite of her extraordinary name, rather drab in attire—at least to be sporting such a garish engagement ring—ought to consider *who* it actually was who might be wanting that baby.

She was scheduled to go into the hospital on her birthday, and on the day before, her parents came up for the festivities, driving up from Westchester in their mustard-colored Subaru. "So, you're twenty-five now," Hills said with some relief, and when she had to admit she'd been saying she was twenty-four because she was *almost* twenty-four, he looked discouraged and tired. Fortu-

nately, her parents, as always, were very polite and atten-
tive and interested in what Hills was doing. She could see
his spirits perking up significantly as he explained, at no
short length, why he hadn't gone to do the show on the
Middle East after "Real World" went off the air. (He had
felt he had made a prior commitment to his psychoana-
lyst, and there was no point in these things unless you
took them seriously. "Oh yes!" her mother had inter-
jected, happy to be off international affairs and on her
own turf.) Then he had launched into a long discussion
of "RIGHT ON!" and the philosophy behind it. He was
the first one to admit, Hills explained, that he hadn't the
background to produce a show for inner-city black kids,
technically speaking, but then, all one needed to be a
good producer, really, was judgment.

"Guess what?" her mother said later in the evening,
reporting back on a suggestion that Lizzie's doctors be
checked out. "Your anesthesiologist is Cricket Chittenden, the wife of your second cousin, once removed!
We've only met her a few times, at funerals and things,
but *everyone* says she is a delight. Your cousin Louzy
Biggs has dinner with them whenever she's in Boston."

As it turned out, everyone *was* right—Cricket Chittenden's anesthesia was a delight, that is, until Lizzie
went under and one second later, or so it seemed, she was
awake and unable to roll over from the pain. But then
they gave her something that made up for everything bad
that had ever happened to her in her life—even for those
lonely weeks at the all girls' boarding school when her
brothers were dropping out of college and into loony
bins—a shot of the blessed, beautiful, glorious morphine.
And then she heard someone whisper, "It looks benign,"
before she sighed herself back to sleep. When she woke
up again, she was in her hospital room with her parents

bustling about, and all she had to do was ring her little bell and someone would shoot her up in the fanny with morphine, every three hours.

"I think she wants a glass of water," she said, finding it more in keeping with things and rather fetching to refer to herself in the third person. The next day her parents had to rush back to Westchester at breakneck speed to open the door for the painters, and she spent the rest of the week spraying herself all over with a powdery cologne called Baby and taking every male visitor who wasn't a blood relation right into her bed. "Chas!" she would say to her new love, the director of "Stage Classics," lifting her weak little arms to draw him down to her fragrant bosom. "William!" to her best friend, whose palm she had never so much as grazed in eleven years of camaraderie. "Just which one of these guys *is* your boyfriend, anyway?" asked her roommate one afternoon—it was her third roommate so far; they seemed to come and go in the flow of things.

She was so happy! Too happy (and too drugged) to care when the eager young intern took it upon himself to tell her, guess what, the tumor could actually be malignant. They wouldn't know for five days. Too happy to concentrate on reading or watching TV; she didn't even need cigarettes anymore! To top it off, she didn't feel like eating a thing! Harry would come to visit every day to eat her hospital dinner. Considering the amount of time her brother had spent in mental hospitals, it was a source of wonder he'd maintained his hankering for institutional food. With Harry's encouragement, she would order up the rice pudding *and* the chocolate cake. And don't forget the soup, Harry would say, perusing the next day's menu. Harry always brought her a carton of Lite n' Lively in spite of her repeated protestations that she didn't even want that. It was nice having Harry visit her in the hospital, instead of the other way around.

Hills made his daily appearance too, after work, but she got the distinct impression that it was quite an ordeal for him, as he always brushed in with the inevitable remark that it was damned hard to park around the hospital. In the midst of it all, Hills had to fly to Kansas City, where his mother had suffered a stroke. "What if I get cancer while you're gone?" she'd said knowing, but not caring, that this was not only inaccurate, but unjust. But while Hills was away they told her it wasn't cancer, and when he returned on her last night at the hospital, he arrived with the shining Sondra and Tye, torn away from that article about electronics, smuggling in a bottle of Beaujolais and four crystal wine glasses.

It was not a wonderful combination, straight morphine and fine wine. Almost immediately she felt a great wave of weepiness welling up inside, as Sondra, in a soft camel sweater, chatted away. Suddenly it occurred to her that Marsha and Sybil had been conspicuously absent on the old sympathy front. They were glad to be rid of her, who could blame them? And yet, it was sad! Though sad for who—Marsha, Sybil, or herself—she wasn't precisely sure, until it hit her with a stab of nausea: Her job contract was running out in July, and *it wouldn't be renewed*. No longer would she be part of the PRV family!

That was all she wanted in life, to be part of the group! With this end in mind, she directed a queasy little smile upon Hills, who was in the midst of making some toast about clear sailing ahead. She didn't know how clear ahead that sailing would be when Hills found out she'd been less than perfectly honest about how great she'd done on those law boards—she hadn't even *taken* the boards, the application form had been returned to her, she couldn't even get her birth date on the right line! She couldn't do anything ("Separate vacations," Hills had said, when she'd confessed she couldn't ski)—not a blessed thing.

Hills was laughing his short, poking snort; he must have made one of his little jokes. "All work and no play makes Hills a dull boy . . . " she could almost hear him thinking. Suddenly she felt a profound, if slightly premature, nostalgia for the nurses who had been so obliging with the hypodermic needle. Despite her groveling, she'd only been able to wheedle a week's prescription for Percodan out of her surgeon. Dear God, where would she be when the drugs ran out, unable to walk for a month, lying around her basement apartment with the view of the fire escape out the bedroom window? Only Hills stood between her and utter disaster. Hills, who was carefully rolling up the wine glasses in a clean dish towel, as Sondra and Tye, laughing, were putting on their coats.

"I wouldn't fucking marry you if you were the last person on earth!" she burst out abruptly, but not without effect. And, as she lay in the suddenly empty room, she wondered, in a detached sort of way, who on earth would be picking her up at the hospital the next morning to go home.

3

"A Man Who Mixed His Pleasure with Pleasure"

Roger still shuddered to think of his last horrifying moments as "Utilization Specialist" for the education department of PRV, going down in flames in front of hundreds of businessmen. It was 1971, his second year on the job, and they'd just finished a project trying to get businessmen to "utilize" TV when he'd gotten the phone call, "Hi Roger, Geo Federal here from Boston Gas . . . " asking him, Roger Stoner, who whenever he saw a bunch of suits thought he was twenty-two again selling life insurance, to speak in front of the New England Chamber of Commerce. He'd tried desperately to talk his way out of it, but then his boss got wind of the idea and thought it was great, simply great. But he had nothing to say to these people, nothing. Well, Roger had thought, I'll look for something to *show* them; after all, *he'd* always liked it in classes when they put on some filmstrip, who even cared what it was, just as long as they clicked off the overhead lights and cranked up the old visual arts projector and allowed you to take a decent nap.

It would have been a great idea, were it not for the fact that all the business programs at PRV were videos and couldn't be projected on a large screen. So Roger ended up bringing the only show he could dredge up that was on film, some training program the education department had tried to push on the police chiefs of Massachusetts—he hadn't been able to bear to put it up on the monitor to take a look ahead of time. How bad could it be? After all, Roger figured, it was just going to be a bunch of businessmen sitting there digesting their cream puff desserts, the last thing they would be looking for was some stimulating "remarks"—no, give these guys a break—and, on Roger's end, well, the film would eat up ten minutes, maybe fifteen.

But when he stood in front of the group, after jocularly opening his talk with the zinger: "Hey! How would you like one day to see the stock board right up there on the screen?" to not so much as a flicker of reaction from the crowd, and then clicked on the projector saying, on a more serious note, "These are the *kinds* of things we do," and up on the screen had come the title "How to Make an Arrest"—he'd broken out in a cold, drenching sweat, exactly as if he had just stepped out of the shower, fully clothed. The only time he'd ever sweated like this was at the Bingham, Boyt, Castaldo (the company he had sold life insurance for) Golf Tournament, where he had gotten rip-roaring drunk at the open bar and then had had to go up to the dais to receive the T-shirt for hitting the longest drive. "Are you all *right*?" said the two guys on the dais flanking him, water *streaming* from the top of his scalp to the tip of his toes, as he'd stood there, unable to stand up without sneaking his hand between the two guys back onto the table behind him for support.

Now Roger stood in the men's room at the North Shore Marriott, the cop film churning away in the function room beyond, tearing off paper towels, jamming them up under his shirt and over his forehead. He had five paper towels stuck to his face when some guy, bored to death with the film, walked in, nodded hello, and then did a double take to see Roger, obviously thinking, Isn't this the guy who's supposed to be up on the dais, making an ass of himself?

He'd picked television because it was the farthest thing from selling life insurance he could think of. He had sold life insurance after college because it had been the expected thing; he had done the expected thing his entire life. He had never rebelled. Or, looking at it from his mother's point of view, he had been "born mature." He had never been depressed. He was "a man who mixed his pleasure with pleasure," to quote the 1963 Exeter yearbook, and a star athlete, elected captain of every team since grammar school. He had never sat around staring at an aquarium hour upon hour, pondering. He was a doer—sometimes, if he wanted to think of something restful when he went to bed, he imagined he was pouring cement in the basement or shoveling a ton of gravel in his driveway.

He'd been such a straight arrow that he'd even gone over to his local draft board on the day after he graduated from college. It was 1967 and he was standing in line at the draft board, all his forms signed, one more check in the right place, and he was in Vietnam. He knew almost nothing about Vietnam—his father would say sometimes: "Rog, why don't you just *glance* at the headlines before turning to the sports page?" But the army hadn't taken him because of his knee. So then, he had had to *think* about his life. What was he supposed to do?

Sell life insurance, everybody had said, with your confidence, you'd be so good at it! But to his surprise, he'd hated it, every single second of it. He'd made a big mistake; he hadn't thought it through, hadn't really thought about it at all. He drifted through his senior year on a sea of beer and almost never, during the various moments of relaxation (what was he relaxing from anyway, the party of the night before?), gone so far as to let his mind rest on what he was going to do with his life. He hadn't even been particularly worried about the very real possibility of flunking out of college, or at least not worried enough to take any corrective action. "Didn't think you'd make it," the dean had said affably as he'd handed Roger his diploma. He'd managed to graduate and then had expected the draft board to take care of his life, even, he supposed, as regarded Jenny Sands.

He would never forget the first time he had laid eyes on Jenny Sands. It was 1963, his freshman year at Dartmouth, and she was a blind date. For all his bravado he would never have dared ask someone so beautiful out. He could still see Jenny Sands coming down the stairs of the dorm of Colby Junior College toward him, her long blond hair flowing to her shoulders with a little bounce upward into its flip, her breasts bursting forth under the white cotton blouse and circle pin, her plaid kilt swirling, just above her knees, held together by that safety clasp that you thought just might somehow get itself accidentally undone with the next prancing step. He had fallen in love immediately, and much later she told him she had rated him as a date with an "A" in her little black book when she was back in the dorm that night.

It had taken him more than a year to get Jenny Sands into the sack, and then afterwards, he'd stayed awake in a rigid position all night because he thought when you loved someone you were supposed to sleep entwined, your arm around her, her head on your chest. Jenny was a good girl, all right—you couldn't say the F-word around Jenny—but she wasn't preppy, not with her divorced mother and washed-up aunts crowded into that dark "garden" apartment in Providence. She was the golden girl who'd come from hell, an All-American girl, prom queen at the public high school, also voted Most Congenial.

He'd gone out with Jenny all through college, through everything that happened. He remembered his sophomore year, the year the hockey team was All-Ivy, getting his father's letter one Saturday morning and tearing off in his car to pick up Jenny and take her to the bar just over the New York border. Later that day they had gone over to someone's house and cooked up some food, and Jenny had wanted to talk to him about the letter. "What's to say? They're getting divorced. What else would you say to that?" Roger had said, and then they'd sneaked off to a room upstairs; she'd thought they were looking for a place to talk, but he'd ended up getting some inside second base. Then a few years later, her mother had committed suicide. Mrs. Sands was a sad case, beaten up by her ex-husband, and Roger could scarcely visualize her now except as being faded, though she must have been good-looking, probably only in her early forties at the time. Roger's mother had given Jenny the news; they were at his mother's house in Connecticut that weekend, since the hockey team was playing against Yale. They'd just come back from the game. Jenny's face had been pink and icy against his cheek as they'd rushed through the front door and down the hall into the pantry to mix the first drink of the day. Afterward, he had driven her to Providence, some fifty miles, without saying a single word.

In Roger's experience if you didn't talk about things they simply went away. He knew he was right on this. The last time he'd felt bad was when he was twelve, comparing the look on his father's face as he opened the front door to Mrs. Ash, his mother's best friend, to his look that Christmas morning when his mother had said, "Come give me a kiss, dear." It was after this elucidating moment that Roger had decided, as a rule, not to think about things, and, he had been happy ever since. He'd tried explaining his views later to Jenny when she'd complained he was "distant" and wanted to talk about their "relationship," or whatever the word for it was back then. "If it's depressing, why talk about it?" had always been his philosophy. Ignore it and it went away. Well, he'd been right, hadn't he? Jenny had simply gone away, a year and a half later. Married the high school boyfriend, Buzz, who had a subscription to *Car and Driver*, someone out of an Archie comic book, for God's sake. In college, it had been love, love, love, but what was supposed to happen after he graduated? Jenny had been desperate to get married and away from those aunts in the dingy apartment. He supposed that even during his senior year, somewhere in the back of his brain had been the question: What was he going to do about Jenny Sands? That year things had not gone well, and even the hockey team, which had been so promising his sophomore year, had been disappointing. He'd been captain, but he hadn't been able to get his teammates, his friends, to change their deadbeat attitude. That was the winter he'd received the long letter from Jenny saying she loved him, she loved him very much. Page after page of Jenny's large, curving handwriting saying that she was sure he would be a success in whatever he did and that she wished him well, but how could she be with someone who never allowed himself, who never allowed her, to talk about anything, ever? That sometimes she would look at him and think he didn't need her or anybody and never would. He'd read the letter, but neither of them had said anything about it, until the following weekend. They were dancing together at a party, and she touched a lump in his breast pocket and asked, "What's that?" And he'd said, "That's the letter you sent me. You're right. I'll try to be better." How they'd both brightened up. That night they'd slept together for the first time in a while, and it had been as good as it had ever been. Everything had been great for the next month or so, but only on the strength of Roger's three sentences, and not for long, because of course, he hadn't changed.

By the time he was selling life insurance, he and Jenny were barely seeing each other. He would call her up every few weeks and they would go out to dinner or a movie and then he would drive her home. They didn't break up completely until the end of the summer. Jenny had gone with him to the wedding of his college roommate, and at the reception she'd turned to him, saying, "I think we should go for a walk."

"Why?"

"Because I don't think we should see each other anymore."

Roger remembered walking down the treelined streets of the pretty neighborhood where his roommate had grown up. It was evening, and the moon was casting shadows on the leaves and the crickets were singing, and Roger was thinking it should have been a nice night for a romantic stroll, but instead they were breaking up. He asked her if she thought she would forget him, eventually forget all about him, even who he was.

"You never forget your first love," Jenny had said, and for an instant, she had made him feel good. When they went back to the reception, someone had pointed a home movie camera at them and Jenny had put on a smiling face, but Roger had turned away, saying, under his breath, "Well, this will be the last picture that will ever be taken of us."

Roger's motto was, "Never look back," but even he was startled by the speed of his recovery. He'd been in love with Jenny Sands for four years and he'd felt bad for one day. Once or twice over the years that followed he'd even wondered briefly, in the detached manner that settled softly upon him after the first six-pack, if maybe something was a little wrong with him that he never suffered.

After Jenny, he'd gone out with the blowsy women that generally came his way, with the odd preppy thrown in. He met most of the women he dated at Brandy's, the bar in downtown Boston where he bartended to support himself while looking for a job in television. You never had to go out on a limb at Brandy's because the girls would come over to you and say, How quick can you get out of here? Even after he got a job at PRV, he still bartended one night a week—Monday was a great night, because on Monday night the people who came in were the people who wouldn't accept that the weekend was over.

At Brandy's, he felt at home, whereas at PRV, in the group of workshirted, Indian-print shawled, committed leftists who worked in the education department, most of whom he might have met ten years before at the Greenwich "Junior Sociables," he felt he stuck out like a sore thumb, showing up for work in the black overcoat from his life insurance–selling days and the Ban-Lon bodyshirts that he had favored in his early twenties, along with the embroidered bell-bottomed jeans and elevated round-toed boots, reminiscent of the Beatles. Truckdriver, hippie, and "Mod Squad" all jumbled up! Even Roger didn't know what he was striving for when something caught his eye in a shop window, except not to be the kind of person who wore a yellow polo shirt or a pair of scuffed Bass Weejuns without socks.

Sometimes he'd arrive at work with his face all bruised and puffy from a hockey game the night before. He was playing a couple of nights each week in a semiprofessional league that was really rough, mostly comprised of French Canadians who had come to cut logs in the mill towns of New England and to take out their anger on the hockey rink at night. By his second season, Roger had made up his mind that, if he was going to continue playing at all, he wasn't going to put up with any more violence for the sake of violence. So one night, when some guy jammed his stick right up between Roger's legs from behind, Roger responded. In one smooth move—after the two of them, more than 400 pounds, had careened against the boards and were bounding back—Roger brought his fist crashing into the side of the guy's head, then hit him again. The referees had pulled him off, but his opponent jumped up, and they fought it out in front of the fans, hardcore, in leather jackets, five thousand of them screaming and going wild—with the result that Roger's team, which had been losing, became fired up and won the game.

I THOUGHT IT WAS TIME TO TEACH HIM A LESSON, STONER SAYS, read the banner headline the next day of the sports page of the *Boston Herald*, a conservative paper not likely to grace the stoop of anyone who worked for WPRV. Or so Roger had prayed as he'd skulked in that morning, his eyes cut up and bruised, his face bandaged in gauze.

This was not to say that the crowd of fervent do-gooders in the education department didn't know how to have a good time. There was more sex going on in that little group than there ever had been on a Sunday night at his Dartmouth fraternity when the official dates had gone home and the girls from the nursing school in town had been brought in. And not just sex, but adulterous sex, wholesomely displayed and viewed tenderly by the group. It was a brand-new concept for Roger, who, during one office party, had stared in disbelief at the sight of Dodge Hornbleu, his wife freshly delivered of their first child the day before, smacking wet kisses upon the slight neck of Leeky Frei, recently hired to fashion "a television bridge" (from what to what?) for single-parented children.

It was his first introduction to the sins of the oh-so-moral that night at that office gathering, a rock 'n' roll party, everyone jammed into Janie Bohn's tiny apartment in Brighton. Janie Bohn! How it happened had taken him completely by surprise. Janie Bohn, a nice girl, a pretty face, really a very pretty face, but very petite, not his type—he'd liked her a lot, in a good-friends-have-a-couple-of-beers-way, she had a great belly laugh for someone so tiny.

He had been going home that weekend to visit his mother in Connecticut and Janie had said be sure and be back in time for the party she was giving that Sunday afternoon, just people from work, and he'd said, "Don't worry. I'll be there, it's a party." He'd slept late that Sunday morning and rushed out of his mother's house without bothering to shave (after all, it was just going to be the crowd from work), without even waiting for his mother to finish making the lunch she had bangingly embarked upon, just grabbing the half-made sandwich and a bottle of beer, and driven the road from Greenwich to Boston on automatic pilot straight to Janie's. It was a great party, as Sunday parties sometimes were, with people drinking too much and dancing. Unfortunately, as it was breaking up, it became clear to Roger that Janie had made the decision that this was to be the party at which she and Roger would get together, because as he was making motions to leave, she kept saying, "No, stay, stay." So he'd stayed, and she came on to him, with that open friendly face turning up to his, and he'd thought, I can't believe this is happening. He'd wanted to say no, but he hadn't known how to without hurting her feelings, so finally he'd said to himself, Well, what the hell?

The next day he'd come into work and there she was, a giant red spot on her face that *he'd* caused by neglecting to shave, and now, as punishment, he would have to watch its progress all week. He had recently made the revolutionary, but still tentative, decision to stop lying to women, so before he had a chance to change his mind, he walked up to her, and said, "We have to talk. What happened last night, well, I think you're great, but I don't think we should have a relationship."

She'd said that she was just appalled that she'd been so presumptuous as to think that he would have the same feelings toward her that she had toward him, and the next day she quit her job to shuck oysters on Nantucket. When he'd thought about it, he just didn't see how he could have done any of it differently.

So why was it he had such trouble bringing himself to sleep with nice, bright, *attractive* (he could hear his mother's voice) Janie Bohn, and yet with Dawn, who wasn't a quarter as interesting, or even as good-looking, Dawn whose conversation-opener was always, "So what's happening, Ro-ga?" there was no problem? Janie simply didn't interest him that way, whereas Dawn did. Of course Dawn *did* have the illustrious distinction of being the only girl Roger had ever gone out with who had decided *while* going out with him to become a hooker. She'd answered an ad in the *Phoenix* placed by a Harvard sociologist who wanted to hire girls at $3.50 an hour to pretend to be prostitutes, in order to interview men who went to prostitutes. After a couple of days, Dawn and a friend had decided it would be more fun to actually turn the tricks. Pepper was her street name.

Not what you would call the PRV type was Dawn/Pepper, though it was through PRV that he'd met her. She was one of the counselors at the community center in Boston where PRV had been shooting "Get Your GED Through TV," the ambitious new program, christened by scores of wine-drenched fund-raisers, to help inner-city kids get their high school equivalencies. The problem was, nobody from the inner city ever showed up, and Roger had to interview Dawn for one entire televised half hour. She was not particularly pretty, and she wore glasses, but she was tall with huge breasts. Oh, she looks interesting, he'd thought to himself, or rather, her breasts looked interesting.

He could never admit this to the nobly promiscuous people he met at PRV, but he'd always liked hookers. With hookers there didn't have to be any pretense of conversation, any pretense of anything at all. He'd gotten his start with hookers, moving straight from the white Maidenform bras of the girls from Greenwich, Connecticut, to the black, lacy contraptions of the twenty-eight-year-old hooker from Beacon Hill—his first year at Exeter. His roommate's father owned the Ritz and Lorenzo, the maître d', had set them up. His roommate had dictated the letter Lorenzo had written the headmaster for permission to have Roger for the weekend: "We thought we'd take the boys for a car ride to

Cape Cod, with a stop along the way for something extra
special to eat . . . "

Even when he'd been in love with Jenny Sands, there'd
been the hooker Buddy Greenstein's uncle had set them up
with when a bunch from the hockey team drove to Florida
over spring break. It had been his sophomore year at Dartmouth; he was Big Man on Campus going with the golden
girl. He and Jenny were officially in love (though they
hadn't slept together yet), and there he was driving over
with Buddy Greenstein, J. J. Bix, Sandy Dey, and Bruce
Manero to some Spanish bungalow, walking with a case of
beer into the kitchen of this woman in a rayon bathrobe
who said, "Guys, I've got a turkey and a ham in the icebox,
help yourself. Who's first?" It had been great—they'd
drawn cards and taken turns and watched TV—and when
he'd told Jenny about it when he returned, she had said,
"Well, I guess that made you a man."

Roger was thirty in 1974 and no longer drove a GTO
or told girls he loved them in order to get them into bed.
He'd shared this revelation with quite a few optimistic
women after his breakup with Jenny Sands. Every time
the muffled, implausible words had escaped his lips,
sometimes without advantage of a second date, he'd
known it was a bad thing to do—but what was done was
done, it was not something upon which he was inclined
to dwell.

Of course, it was no longer necessary to tell women
you loved them in 1974, particularly if you were a producer at a public television station, where it was considered dishonest not to sleep with someone if he or she was
of the opposite sex and there was the slightest attraction.
Now women came to him in the darkness of editing
rooms or at a friend's house on the Cape when there

weren't enough beds to go around. Everyone was very grown-up; sleeping with a new person was part of life, like eating a meal at an unfamiliar restaurant. Not quite as exciting as in the old days, maybe—but then you were bound to lose in excitement for what you gained in the ease of the transaction. He was a great believer in being rational and had invented his own system of going out with women, weekends only, on a seasonal basis. In the winter, it might be skiing with Deb DeFranco, and then when the snow melted it was on to Cindy Hoops, who looked great in a bikini. This made perfect sense to him. After all, there was no guarantee you were going to *marry* a girl who was going to ski well, so why not *go out* with a girl who skied well? Of course, he acknowledged, there was no guarantee he was going to marry anyone at all. He'd always assumed, however vaguely, that he would get married someday. Everybody got married. Still, sometimes he wondered why of all the girls he'd dated, Jenny Sands was the only one he had ever truly cared about.

Once, at a Celtics game, he thought he saw her sitting in the front row. At the half he raced down, but of course, he'd found himself staring into the face of a startled stranger. Another time he'd actually thought of calling her up to find out what had happened to her. But then he realized he didn't even know where she lived. Besides, what was the purpose? He knew if he'd married her, he'd be divorced by now. He didn't know why he knew that, but he was certain it was true.

A few times, in the year he turned thirty, he had come home alone after a night of drinking and found himself starting to cry, not about Jenny, not about anyone, just for no reason at all. He couldn't remember having cried since he'd sliced his foot open on a broken bottle at age ten and chanted to himself that "soldiers don't cry."

Twenty years later, he still didn't see the point in crying. So he'd simply poured himself a stiff scotch and gone straight to bed, falling asleep, as he always did, no matter what had happened in the course of the day, within thirty seconds of his head hitting the pillow. It was his greatest gift.

4

Three Meaningful Relationships

"But you don't *have* cancer!" her father said. "You should be happy!"

"You don't understand," Lizzie said, bursting into tears again, "my life is over!" and so it seemed to be as she withdrew from the morphine, and for the next two days she cried and cried, as her father, with the fortitude of a soldier, strode back and forth across Mass Ave. to the Sears department store, holding up his palm with an official air against the endless stream of cars, in order to return once again the window shades that refused to go up.

"Don't you want me to stay and help?" her father said weakly the third day when she pleaded with him to go home. "Your mother thinks you need someone to take care of you." But the window shades lying in creased heaps on the floor and her inexplicable misery were not without their persuasions. By 10:00 A.M., he had kissed her good-bye, and from the window she watched him nestling happily into his seat, reaching to the glove compartment to pop into his mouth the Baby Ruth bar that all her life ("Is Daddy home yet?" she would ask and ask her mother, who'd thought such devotion so touching) had always been there.

Naturally she had wished to be alone when it was the worst possible time to be alone. It was difficult to walk; the pain caused her to shuffle along like a little old lady bent in two. When she'd hobbled into the converted closet that was her kitchenette, she'd discovered how it was her brother Spencer, who had stayed in her apartment the week she was in the hospital, could live on $2,000 a year, in that the icebox was empty and in the one plastic cupboard she found only Wheaties and peanut butter.

She wasn't due back at work for a month. And so she lay in her sandbox of a bed, almost inserted into the TV set that sat upon her pillow, watching hour upon hour of reruns of "Bonanza" and "December Bride"—sometimes drifting off into dreams of herself in a long pink hostess gown slamming the shiny door of Hills's sedan as they dashed off evanescently to yet another party. As for the real Hills, who'd mentioned when she'd called that he was a bit under the weather and would be keeping a low profile, he'd kept a profile so low that he'd effectively dropped out of sight. Now that she couldn't have him, of course, she desperately wanted him back.

I'll see him when I get back to the station, she'd thought comfortingly to herself. Hills couldn't escape her there, not if he was ever to pee again, as the "RIGHT ON!" offices were just around the corner from her office and used the men's room one door down from where she typed her transcripts. In fact, there was no way for Hills even to get to his office without passing her, short of leaping up one story over the balcony. And yet, when she finally returned to the station in May (to the tepid reception of Marsha and Sybil, who had tidied up her work area leaving behind no trace of her former frazzled existence), she found Hills evincing more passion in his avoidance of her than ever he had evinced in their affair. Indeed, it was a testimony to the power of Hills in the field of urine retention that she was not to lay eyes upon him once in a full month after she was back at work— unless her instincts were correct about the tiny edge of blue workshirt she saw flapping wildly one day around the corner.

Then it was June, and flowers were blossoming and the days lengthening and the yearnings for love that had always filled the air at PRV hung so heavily you could scarcely breathe, and Lizzie would race home at lunch hour to collapse in a puddle of tears. In less than two months her job contract would expire and she would be leaving the station! And yet, she was not entirely without hope. For soon the PRV auction would come, disrupting all programming, the PRV auction that ever since she was a child living in Concord where everyone was so *involved*, had filled her with such a celebratory feeling— how she had admired Mrs. Andrews sitting on the phone on TV! For ten days all regular jobs at the station were to be suspended, and she would be working strange, romantic hours as a production assistant in the studio with all the cute directors and crew. And the climax was the big all-night party, starting at midnight on the final evening when all joined together in exhausted camaraderie!

But she had nothing to wear; she was still overweight

from her month lying in bed. At first the operation had been everything she'd dreamed of in terms of losing weight. That week in the hospital, she had not needed to smoke, to eat, even to talk. She had felt herself drifting, drifting to the purity that had always been Spencer's and never hers. She had not been able to avoid a little self-congratulation right in the middle of her spirituality. You are really something, girl, she had said to herself. Then had come her first week home from the hospital, when she'd been denied the shots of straight morphine, and down Mass Ave. she'd crawled at 3:00 A.M. to Dunkin' Donuts for a quick dozen.

So, in the blind hope that the right clothes would make the weight go away, she'd bought herself a white lacy dress with ruffles down the front.

Thus it was as a wedding cake that she appeared to be PA the last night of the auction—how lucky she was to be assigned that night so she could be part of the "wrap" party. She arrived with an expectant air and got to work (she hadn't a clue what she was supposed to do; luckily nobody asked her to do anything) next to Chas as director—Chas, with the moistened eyes, to whom she had yielded up the last vestige of her virtue one afternoon of her convalescence! Chas, married, with a girlfriend at the station; how shocked Lizzie would have been if she could have foreseen that moment six months before. Back in the fall, she'd had trouble with the idea that people in real life committed adultery; still, she hadn't been able to help wondering if Chas's having a girlfriend made her crush more futile or less so. But on that rainy April afternoon, none of it had mattered. Lying on top of her bed in her forlorn apartment, dressed down to her shoes, with too brightened cheeks, like the sick girl in *Heidi*, it had been like taking candy from a baby. She was so grateful to be gathered up in his arms, so happy for those few moments not to be alone. "I'm fat, you know," she'd warned him as he unbuttoned her shirt.

"Oh, Lizzie, I don't care," said Chas heroically, and she'd said a prayer of thanks to the touchy-feely warmth of the liberals at WPRV that called fat superficial and adultery an honest expression of feeling.

But now, on the last night of the auction, apparently they were just good friends, and at this climactic event, that was supposed to be filled with such magic, Chas had been preoccupied with his directing and not talked much to her.

But then, just as she was sinking into defeat, up on the screen in the control room appeared Roger Stoner—full of life, striding about and going on a mile a minute about why one should pledge money to WPRV—and suddenly hope came back into the world.

"Roger Stoner is *so* attractive," Sybil had told her in September, as Lizzie had left the station with William to go over to Roger Stoner's for a newsroom party. Why, she had wondered later, as William and she walked through a Victorian living room with a green-and-mustard geometric rug, were they going down into the basement? But when she'd descended and seen the purple plywood bar and Ping-Pong table, and Roger lounging on a couch in short hair and an awful paisley shirt, it had all fit in. He was everything she detested in a guy: athletic, assured, and unscrewed-up. She had heard he had gone to Dartmouth; probably he had drunk beer there. A shallow jock! She had ignored him hotly all evening, listening instead to Tom Koch, a reporter and the most beautiful man she'd ever seen, talk to William at great length about how much money William's ex-girlfriend had, a topic that seemed to fill Tom with great fire.

Her one direct encounter with Roger that night had been a drunken run-in over playing old Beatles records—she still liked the Beatles and had kept true to her preteen vow to never like the Rolling Stones—when Roger, as host, had actually had the nerve to suggest changing *Beatles '65* (which, thanks to her fierce diligence, had played three times running on side two) to something people could dance to. And later, when William had asked her if she wanted to go out drinking with Roger and him, she had triumphantly said no, *he* of course should feel free to go if he were really so inclined, but to please, *please* drive her home first.

But then recently, back at work after her operation, she'd felt her prejudice lifting. As she'd directed her head-phone-framed face supplicatingly down the Hills-less hall-way—in the hope of finding someone to bring home to her bachelorette apartment so she wouldn't be stuck chat-ting with the two MIT grads from across the hall who pranced over as their stereo blasted, doing "The Pony"—she'd felt rising within her a universal love of mankind. And as Roger rushed by, completely unaware of her exis-tence, she'd thought, here was the only person at WPRV who didn't smile back, didn't even notice her, was so engrossed in his work that he didn't seem to be interested in flirting—a phenomenon at WPRV! Even old weighed-down-with-the-responsibilities-of-the-world Hills (who'd actually had his secretary call to invite her to a dinner party in the period she was still sleeping with him) had always found time to stop and chat, or at least until he'd had to flee her.

But now on the control-room monitor was a com-pletely different image of Roger than the work-absorbed one she'd come up with. This one was far closer to the mark, nearer the puppy-dog range she generally preferred—cute, with an adorable (as opposed to tough, when he walked down the hallway) semicircular scar under his right eye, and for a moment, just an instant, he looked like her father, and in that moment, she was afraid to admit, she fell for Roger Stoner.

She'd never bought all that Freud stuff—not that she had ever read Freud, of course, but everybody knew the gist—and while she certainly loved her father, search as she could, she never could find even a teensie bit of lust for him. Happily, the various shrinks she had seen had never bothered with her father, either; they'd been too engrossed in her screwed-up brothers, who had set the tone for most of her boyfriends. But oddly what attracted her to Roger was the opposite of what was true of the brothers: his stability and authority, the way he cleared his throat that made you think he probably had a bunch of coins jingling in his pockets.

But she was just an overweight secretary in a wedding-cake dress, sitting there purposelessly in the control room, when suddenly during a break Roger swung in, grabbed from her hand the cigarette she had just lifted from the pack, deftly twirled it around his fingers while mockingly scrambling for matches, struck a match while flicking the twirling cigarette into his mouth, lit the cigarette, took one dramatic, addictlike drag, and then passed it back to her. Her heart was *pounding* with excitement, but before she could muster a response to these antics, he was gone, as quickly as he had appeared. She sat wondering in a rare realistic moment why she had ever thought anything would ever work out the way it was supposed to be.

At ten o'clock her shift ended. She didn't know how to fill the two hours before the party, and suddenly she felt terribly alone. Her most frequent nightmare was that she was on a hill by herself, and the sky was like a TV screen on the fritz, streaked with black and gray horizontal lines. She didn't care that the world was ending, she just wanted to get over to the neighboring hill where all sorts of people who knew her (but, admittedly, didn't seem to care) were milling about.

She drove home.

5

Another Meaningful Relationship

As it happened, when she ran off with Roger Stoner four weeks after the PRV auction, she was already in love till death do them part with someone else.

It was Tom Koch! The beautiful reporter she had met at Roger Stoner's newsroom party back in September. Tom Koch, who was not simply way beyond her in the looks department, but married besides. She didn't know how to describe him, he was so breathtaking. Of course she shouldn't have *had* to describe him, because the whole thing was dead secret, unless you put two and two together when you saw them having lunch every single day at PRV, engaged in long, intense conversation. Tom was still in his twenties but he looked more like a grown-up man than Hills in his late thirties—he didn't wear the uniform of PRV, but expensive shirts and ties. His yellow hair swept back off his face, and when he smiled, a badly chipped tooth completed his perfection by its imperfection. The men hated him, and the women parted when he passed. Even the impeccable Sondra, who for some reason was the one and only one brought into their confidence, was impressed. "But how will you entertain for him?" she sometimes worried.

At first, when Tom plunked his tray down on the table beside hers, with searing questions about life, it was inconceivable that this was flirtation. Suddenly she felt strong and in control, returning home after work every night (after, it must be admitted, a rousing, eye-locking lunch with Tom—what *had* they been discussing so fervently?) to her Jane Austen novels and her cup-measured dinner of cottage cheese and Birds Eye Italian Green Beans.

She had moved back to 441 Harvard Street (Boo having suddenly moved out) at the end of May, and the next day had simply turned to the girl next to her in the cafeteria line at PRV and said, "Would you like to move into my apartment?" Tina was a quiet woman who worked for the newsroom as an associate producer. She was twenty-five and was still living with her parents, although Lizzie, who had just learned her name the day before, hadn't known even this rather major detail about her life. Through dumb luck, Tina agreed to move in, and with her had come her father and two brothers to paint her bedroom and sand her windowsill down to the wood. For a lark, Lizzie set Tina up with Cobb, the brother of a friend, a guy so quiet you couldn't hear him when he moved about. Soon he was over every night, pitching in on that windowsill, when he wasn't making bread in the kitchen.

Tina and Cobb never talked—Lizzie would just hear the gentle rock of the table under the kneading of bread or the scrape-scrape-scrape of sandpaper until 9:00 P.M., when like clockwork they wandered into Lizzie's room, where she would be reclining on the bed surrounded by six empty cans of Tab, and stood expectantly in front of her as if she were their favorite show on television. Then, after an hour of Lizzie regaling them with stories about herself, it was lights out for all, or so she assumed, until one particularly Tab-ridden night, she got up at 1:00 A.M. to use the bathroom and noticed the light on in the kitchen, and there was Cobb kneading away at a couple of lumps of dough. "But Cobb!" she cried out, "There are six loaves in the freezer!"

"I know," said Cobb with a sad shake of his head, "I'm just afraid we'll run out."

Lizzie too worried about the future. She and Tom had a serious discussion. Her PRV contract was up July 31, and here was an opportunity, Tom said, to get out of this ridiculous television business, and focus on getting a paralegal job while she was applying to law school. Although she didn't have the heart to tell Tom about her former endeavors in the law board application arena, she wholeheartedly agreed. Feeling very focused about her career one Saturday, she went over to Saks and wandered by accident into the designer section. Like a scene from a movie (except for the fact they wouldn't accept her check with her driver's license as I.D. because it had expired— "But it's still me!" she had cried), she emerged transformed in an expensive swinging dress.

She had to admit there were still a few minor problems with Tom, number two being he was married, number one being there was nothing whatsoever going on between them. As a result, she felt obligated to keep up some kind of token effort in the Roger Stoner offensive. Not that she hadn't been tempted to throw in the towel after the PRV softball debacle, when, on the basis of overhearing in the cafeteria someone saying, "I hope Stoner's playing tonight, we could use some home runs," she'd gone out and bought shorts and sneakers, then parked in a tow-away zone near the softball field—only to find that Roger Stoner hadn't come and who *had* come were some muscley-looking girls whizzing fastballs at one another.

Dutifully she made one last effort early in July, making William, who already had a date, bring her along to a newsroom party. The first thing she'd heard when she'd arrived was the host at the stove, saying to someone or other, "Stoner's in Connecticut visiting his mother," and her heart sank. But then, through the kitchen door, still in his seersucker suit, who should walk in but Tom—who had said he wasn't coming—and without his wife. She was so happy, even after William had darted her a look and said, "There's that asshole." Tom had walked up to her, stirred the chili once and said, glowering at the bottom of the pot in a kind of Rebel-Without-a-Cause manner, "Let's get out of here," and out she'd scurried—with William, to whom she confided every detail of her daily life, whispering loudly behind, "Don't go with him!" and Lizzie whispering back to William, "It's *none* of your business," in a highly grown-up manner, as she jumped into the car next to Tom.

In the car, Tom was silent and tormented. "What number Harvard Street?" he finally said, thrillingly. As they walked up the dusky hallway stairs, she felt exactly as if she were in a 1940s movie, if you didn't count the shoulder pad traveling across her neck. Tom hadn't said a single word since he'd asked where she lived. It was *terribly* exciting. It was also early in the evening, and Tina was still at the newsroom party, so they would be alone. She fumbled with the key in the door, walked straight into her room, and sat on the edge of her bed while Tom proceeded to pace up and down. During their long intellectual conversations (Tom would always start things with, "Let's make an agenda") he had always looked her directly in the eye: now he looked everywhere but.

"There's A and then B, and there's A and then C," Tom blurted out abruptly, breaking the steamy silence. Sweet baby Jesus. Had she missed something? She didn't know. She didn't care. Her heart was throbbing. She was leaping to the surety that he must like her *that way.*

"We're at A now. If we go to B, we can never return to A," Tom continued, "but, if we *stay* at A for now, when the time is right, we can go straight to C." He met her eyes. Lizzie nodded as if she knew what they were deciding. Then, without another word, he was gone.

What, had she been proposed to?

6

The Miracle

Lizzie felt she had been very patient. Certainly her love for Tom was deep, even though the moment they had decided to do the noble thing, the whole "affair" (never had that word seemed appropriate until now, when she wasn't actually having an affair) had become seedy, with meeting for lunches clandestinely—except Tom could never decide which restaurant. There would be six phone calls in the morning on where to meet, with Tom singularly unamused by her handicap when it came to directions, and they would end up taking separate cars and rendezvousing in dangerous intersections on the highway, with barked instructions for Lizzie to follow Tom to large businessman restaurants (where presumably nobody from WPRV would be caught dead) that served surf and turf and salad with iceberg lettuce. Their entire relationship became mired in Tom's obsessive agonizing over logistics—by the time they managed to get together he would be looking at his watch while she peeled the label off the ginger ale bottle.

Still, she felt that when love was real it was worth

waiting for. And yet . . . it had been *three whole weeks* since Tom had proposed the noble pact of going from A to C (a pact that might have united them in its virtuousness, had its pronouncement not been followed soon thereafter by rather "B-ish" grapplings in the front seat of Tom's car) and he still hadn't left his wife! In fact, one night he'd actually invited Lizzie over to one of his wife's dinner parties. She'd been so taken aback she'd had to ask two times if it was really Tom at the other end of the phone.

But *was* she going to marry Tom? Well certainly not now after what she'd done at William's birthday party, when she'd flung any possibility of a relationship between Tom and her to the winds like a handful of confetti. Had her behavior that night been prompted by self-survival, or by the good old self-destructive instinct she had always been able to call her friend? She supposed, in the final analysis, she had just been drunk.

Certainly she had been drunk. In front of everyone: Tom and his wife (he'd warned Lizzie she was coming; still, it had been a shock to see her); William, of course, ever watchful and disdainful of all her relationships with men; even Spencer and Harry had been there—Spencer to guard her virtue and Harry to help her throw it away.

But she hadn't cared. She was unemployed (as of close of work that day) and it was too hot, still 115 degrees at 8:00 P.M. Her meticulously hot-combed hair was already beginning to rise up against its enforced sleekness, her new dress was sticking to her legs, her makeup sliding down her face. There had been no time to waste. She had strode into William's party, with a brave abandon, bound for she knew not what—except, of course, the fortification of the wine table. Quickly, she had dashed down four plastic cups of wine, holding her breath against the taste; within seconds the alcohol had hit her system with the sudden rush of an intravenous drug. Only then did she allow herself a moment to survey the terrain. There near the window, by the grace of God, stood Roger Stoner, deep in conversation with the executive producer of the news. With a sigh, she glided toward the two men, appearing with a little bounce between them as if from the air. Surprised, they stopped their conversation, which had been quite animated, and turned to her in polite expectation.

"Don't mind me," she said with a beatific smile, "I'm just going to stand here and pretend I'm talking to you."

By now Roger knew who she was ... he *thought.* Actually, he wasn't positive, even though he must have run into her a hundred times. When he'd first met her back in September he had supposed she was William's girlfriend, and, judging by her actions, an ass. She had arrived with William for one of his newsroom parties in a skirt up to her navel. He had appreciated the outfit, until she had proceeded to practically accost him at the record player when all he wanted to do was change the Beatles record that had been playing half the night to something you could dance to. Then later when the party was breaking up, he'd said to William, "Let's hit some bars, but, Jesus, can you get rid of that girl?"

Later on he found out she was Spencer Reade's little sister. What next? Everytime you looked Spencer Reade had some relative getting let out for the day. Like the guy last fall with the wild white hair who was *incredibly* famous (to everyone, evidently, but Roger) who'd been allowed to leave the mental hospital to do a live broadcast of his poetry and instead had accidentally locked himself into the men's room for the hour. And then there

was Harry, whom Roger had only just met that winter
when he'd come over to Roger's house to watch a Bruins
game. William had called and asked if he could bring
along Spencer and Harry—and he'd said sure, and made
up a large plate of tuna sandwiches, plenty for four
grown men, he'd thought. Then Harry had walked
through the door and proceeded to dispense with the
entire plate, without taking his coat off or interrupting
his unceasing monologue about how he, Harry, didn't
drink or take drugs anymore, not that he was *morally*
opposed or anything, but because all they did was either
make him sleepy or hungry—in fact he'd had just *one*
glass of wine the night before and had woken up so
sleepy that morning he hadn't planned on coming to
Roger's, but then suddenly he'd gotten a second wind.
Who asked? Roger had wanted to say, and yet he'd liked
Harry, had liked him as soon as his lumbering frame had
come through the door.

No, he'd never been much interested in the girl—
except for one time, recently, when he'd run into her
again. They had just happened to be walking up the
loading ramp at the same time, and suddenly he hadn't
been able to keep his eyes off her. She was chatting away
with this incredible sparkle in her eyes, striding up the
ramp in a swank, sexy summer dress, not like those
robes, or whatever it was women seemed to clothe themselves with at PRV, and she'd had this energy about her
that was different, too. Her car keys had fallen down
some crevice or something, he didn't know, she'd been
talking away, laughing. But it had only been a moment.
They'd gone their separate ways, and he'd pretty much
forgotten about her. Not that he would have dreamed of
calling her up, in any event.

But now, here she was, just standing there next to

him beaming away, as relaxed as if they'd known each other all their lives. And this after she'd come over and planted herself decisively between two people she barely knew, as if she had something terribly important to communicate, and then, it turned out, she had absolutely nothing to say, not even a "Gee, it's hot, isn't it?" Not the merest pretense of something to say. This apparently hadn't bothered her in the slightest. In fact nothing seemed to bother her. Apparently, she hadn't an ounce of embarrassment in her. When a little later on they were laughing about something, she suddenly announced she had to get more wine, and when she turned around, he noticed the back of her silk dress. "Hey," he had said, "did you know that you have a huge wine stain down the back of your dress?" He had expected her to be aghast, to go and run and throw some water on it, at the very least. Sometimes his mother spent a week working on a stain, soaking and scrubbing some rag of a garment that would have been rejected by Goodwill. But instead she had said, "Yes, I know and I'm rather proud of it," mockingly giving her disheveled mass of hair a little pat, as if she were a high-fashion model, as she'd teetered away. For this, he couldn't help but feel respect. But it wasn't until later, when she tried to sit on top of the hedge, that he was truly moved.

It was, Roger supposed, nearly 4:00 A.M. by then and still hotter than hell. He was standing on the front porch chatting away with William and having a drink, very convivial, as if it were only the start of a summer's evening, instead of the fourteenth drink into it. They'd just finished off a joint to liven things up. It had been an auspicious move, William had said, possibly brilliant. Philosophically speaking, he and William agreed completely, meaning they both liked to drink. Serenely they stood side by side on the cramped, rickety front porch of the three-decker house, surveying like lords of the manor the tiny brown patch of scrub yard before them.

"Might I 'freshen' your drink?" Roger asked William most politely ("Now Roger," his aunt Cornelia had told him once, "never say, 'Do you want *another* drink, Aunt Cornelia,' say, 'May I *freshen* that drink for you, Aunt Cornelia,' or, 'Would you care for a little *soupçon?*'")— as he sloshed William a huge splash of wine from the half-gallon jug he had grabbed on their way through the house. It was at this point that Lizzie suddenly reappeared from nowhere—throughout the evening she'd been appearing and disappearing. The last time he'd seen her, through a haze of cigarette smoke, Tom Koch had been adhesive-taping her wrists to the doorhandle of the refrigerator—"That's the stupidest fucking thing I've ever seen," he seemed to remember remarking casually to Tom Koch's wife, as they'd stood swaying in the doorway looking placidly on.

Now here she was again, with a little determined look on her face, her hair frizzing up a foot around her head, navigating her way past them, with nary a hi, how are you, down the front walk in high heels, her body lurching over to the grass and back again to the broken cement walk, in the general direction of the privet hedge.

Roger lost himself marijuanally in the huge deep plum stain that made a geographical configuration on the back of her dress. It had begun as Maine but dried surprisingly to something more approaching Nebraska. He and William watched her in silent complacency as she finally reached the spare, but neatly manicured, hedge and began, with the concentration of a dog circling round to mat down imaginary grasses, carefully positioning herself to sit on top of it. He couldn't believe she was actually going to try and sit on the hedge—even a child knew you couldn't sit on a hedge! Clearly rationality was *not* a consideration here. It was ridiculous, yet he couldn't help but admire her, because something inside of him had always wanted to sit on one of those pruned hedges, though *everyone* knew you would simply crash down through the scratchy branches to the dirt below.

He and William watched as Lizzie crashed through the scratchy branches to the dirt below.

Early on in the evening she had had to give up all pretense of being lovely and demure. She had been dead drunk within a half hour of arriving (and meeting Tom Koch's wife), but had not let that interfere with further drinking. Twice in the middle of conversation, she had suddenly fallen into a sitting position on the floor, her legs stretched out neatly in front of her. By the time she was headed for the hedge, there had been nothing to do but hope for a miracle. Finally it had come: Roger Stoner had scooped her up from the bushes and taken her in to dance, brambles in her hair. She closed her eyes when he first kissed her a few moments later. When she opened them, the cops were there.

Tina and Cobb were listening to classical music when she burst into her apartment at 9:00 A.M., the pink dress mangled from the banks of the Lincoln Reservoir, where she had sat, ankles crossed, politely watching Roger Stoner take every last stitch of his clothing off. How this had exactly transpired she wasn't sure. After the cops (summoned by the neighbors to protest the noise but finding only Roger and her) had left, Roger had murmured, "Wouldn't it be more comfortable at my house?" Where had Roger been all these years coming up with a line like that? It was actually quite endearing. Still, she had her morals. No, no, she'd said, absolutely no, not on the first date, if you could call making out on William's beige velour sofa a date.

She'd been rather pleased at her forcefulness, she had been becoming quite smug about it, and then Roger had said, how about a swim? Practically the next thing she knew there he was wet, nothing on, walking up the shore to her, as she carefully examined a clump of grass under her right hand. What was she supposed to do? On the one hand, she'd been trying to not sleep with him on some kind of principle, though she wasn't sure exactly which one, considering she herself was an adulteress; on the other hand, she'd felt bad that, in those natural times, she hadn't been "free" enough, unashamed of her body enough, to have thrown off all her clothes and gone swimming with him. In the end, she supposed, it didn't much matter to the world what she did. She'd opened her arms to him.

She gave a little wave to Tina and Cobb, went into the bathroom, and passed out in a cold tub. It was still over a hundred degrees. She woke up with a start—she'd never fallen asleep in a tub before, and she wondered absently why she hadn't drowned. She got out, and then remembered all the towels were four flights away, mildewing in the washer where she'd forgotten them the day before. She had once tried to dry herself with a piece of toilet paper, a bitter failure (the toilet paper had rubbed into little balls at the first enthusiastic swipe). This time she poured baby powder all over herself as a kind of blotting device. Then the question was: Should she chance it that Cobb was safely kneading bread in the kitchen and dash out of the bathroom naked into the hallway and into her room? She decided to go for it. She raced out into the hallway, just as the front door was opening to Tina's entire family, dressed in old clothes and armed with sandpaper, and ran into her room leaving white powdered footprints behind her. Then the doorbell rang. When Tina answered it, she blinked twice. It was her boss.

"Hi," Roger said. "Is Lizzie home?" and off Lizzie and Roger drove to her parents' cabin in New Hampshire, where the brothers were for the weekend, breaking every rule the parents had ever made.

7

The First Fight

They hadn't spent a night apart since they'd stayed up
all night at William's sweltering party and ended up,
after a swim, at HoJo's at 7:00 A.M. Here, amidst a hundred clamoring kids and parents who had just crawled
gasping from fitful sleep out of Winnebagos in the parking lot, Lizzie had demurely ordered *hot* oatmeal in her
torn pink dress, as if it were the most natural thing in
the world to order at one hundred degrees in the morning. What were you going to do with a girl like that, but
stick around to see what happened next? It wasn't as if
he'd given it any thought; one thing had just led to
another. First it was a night, then it was a weekend in
New Hampshire, then it was a week in Bermuda. "So,
where are we going to celebrate our one week's anniversary?" Roger had said that first Sunday as they were
lounging around the cabin, and off they'd driven from
New Hampshire straight to Crimson Travel. At the airport, she'd bought a cheap ring, ripping the fake jewel
off as they were boarding, and flaunted it all week at the
hotel, green on her finger.

They'd had a great time, then they'd come home and he'd gone back to work, getting as involved as always—except that every afternoon around three he'd find himself thinking, Gee, better call Lizzie and see what's up. What was up would be that Lizzie was in the middle of cleaning out her drawers or some other hopeless task of the unemployed, and this would segue into, So what are we doing tonight? Then over she would come in that junkbox of a car (which, it turned out, had only thirty thousand miles on it—it just *looked* like it had a hundred and fifty), arriving with a great big Cheshire Cat grin on her face, as if she'd just made it through a war zone and was thrilled to be alive. They'd go out, stay home—it didn't matter what they did. He'd seen her every day for what, a month, two months? Well, why not, they were having a great time.

Since he was a teenager having a great time had become something of a point of honor. It ran in the family. Even his mother, with all her high standards, had flunked out of Vassar her freshman year because she'd been going to too many tea dances. In the darkest days after the divorce, she'd dragged herself from bed, trimmed the tree, and invited the usual crowd in for bourbon and eggnog. Why *not* have a good time? he wanted to know. He pretty much had a good time 365 days a year. "See this glass of water?" he'd said once when asked how this could be, then drunk it with a tremendous gusto. "Best glass of water I ever had."

It was on the basis of this philosophy that he had taken Lizzie to Logan's party one Monday night. It wasn't as if he didn't know it would be a bad party; it was just something to do on a Monday night when there was nothing else to do. Logan was a guy from his fraternity in college, a sad SOB whose parties were always a mission to get people to like him. When they'd arrived—Roger, Lizzie, and William, who'd come along because why not?—there were bowls of rolled joints laid on coffee tables, the way his parents used to set out cigarettes before cocktail parties, and kegs of beers and gallons and gallons of ice cream sitting in trash-cans filled with ice. Jesus, the guy was pathetic.

Roger had never really cared for these so-called wild fraternity parties, even when he was in a fraternity. There was always some guy like Logan who thought dropping your pants and throwing moons was hilarious instead of plain disgusting. Or a guy like Moakely, the strongest guy at Dartmouth (and that was strong), who during one frat party had bent down when Jenny Sands was dancing and bitten her on the ass. That had been in the basement of the fraternity house; Roger had been upstairs where he was lead singer and drummer of "Dusty Dingle and the Berries," a lackadaisically assembled musical group whose chief talent lay in not playing a single note until late in the evening, right before everybody passed out. (The next day, people would either say, "Hey the band was *great* last night," or "Gee, did you guys play last night?") Roger hadn't heard about the biting until fifteen minutes after it happened, at which point he'd gone screaming down the stairs and slammed all 250 pounds of Moakely against the concrete wall and said, "If you ever do any-thing like that again, I'll kill you." He'd meant it, and Moakely had skulked away. He'd been pretty surprised at himself at the time; he'd never been into the macho thing of fighting guys. Except for the incident on the hockey rink, he'd never even had a fistfight.

They hadn't been at Logan's two minutes when, way-laid at the bar, he looked across the crowded room and saw Logan, his total idiot sorry-assed self, sauntering up to Lizzie. Well, Roger thought, there you see the two most unlike people you'd ever want to meet—no, he didn't quite think they'd be hitting it off with some rollicking discussion of English literature in the very near future, but what was he worried about, how bad could it be? Still, he had started on his way to rescue Lizzie when he saw it was too late: Logan had embarked on the "Beer Swizzle," a particularly unfunny (even for Logan) joke where he would take a big sip of beer, then go over and start talking to someone—isn't this a great band, etc.—then slowly let the beer trickle out of the corner of his mouth. Roger motioned to Lizzie to join him if she wanted, and then went on to say hello to a friend. About five minutes later she'd come jostling through the crowd up to him and just erupted, without having said a single word in warning, let alone started an argument. "What's the problem?" he said. "To hell with him. *We're* having a good time."

"That's *it!*" she said through clenched teeth. She was boiling over. "I'm *walking* home!"

"You can't, it's three miles!" he said, but she'd stomped off anyway, and so he'd gone up to William, who, undeterred by the minor fact that he didn't know a soul in the place, was chatting away, a beer in one hand, a joint in the other. "Listen," Roger said, "Lizzie's all bent out of shape, she's walked out, and she's insisted she's going to walk home, so go grab her, will you, and get her off the street."

"What?" said William, and then shrugged and went after her.

After William left, Roger only stayed another half hour. There were an awful lot of men at the party, hardly any women, not that he was looking. He went home, brushed his teeth, got in bed, and was asleep, midair, before his head hit the pillow.

*   *   *

He wasn't going to call? He wasn't even going to call? She couldn't *believe* he wasn't going to call. She'd been sitting on her bed and staring at her clock for hours. Was this the end? She didn't even know what had happened; something had just suddenly possessed her, some kind of frustration. She hadn't a single clue what had so enraged her, not to say, of course, that she didn't feel she had *clearly* been in the right. Well, maybe not *clearly*—it certainly would have strengthened her point, knowing what it was. But none of it mattered; now all she felt was sick inside. They'd been together every night for seven and a half weeks. It had been going so well. She had felt that the "I love you" that she always waited for the guy to say first would be popping out of his mouth, him liking it or not, any day now. Now she had this terrible suspicion that if they were apart one night it would be all over, the chain broken, the momentum dissipated. She waited for him to call through three more cigarettes. Why had she gotten so mad? It wasn't as if he'd been flirting or anything; Roger never flirted. She'd just suddenly been filled with rage. The party had represented everything she hated, a bunch of beer-drinking fraternity jocks who'd never had a deep, sensitive thought about anything, a group she'd hotly eschewed all her life, and had so desperately tried not to think of as being associated with Roger. The stereotype *was* true, after all! All Dartmouth guys did *was* get drunk and talk about the last time they'd been drunk! Not, of course, that she herself wasn't known to personally tie one on now and then, but there was a *big* difference, a very big difference indeed, she just happened to be too drunk at the moment to be able to articulate it. Anyway, *now* what did it matter? She wanted Roger, she didn't care what he was, he wasn't really that, anyway. She was sick, sick, sick. It was

5:00 A.M. *He wasn't going to call.* She supposed she was still drunk. She got out of bed and reeled down the stairs and out the door to her car.

He was awoken out of deep sleep to what, *pebbles* on his window? He stumbled in his underwear to the back door and opened it. There she was, her hair a mile high in the early morning mist. He hadn't thought about her, or really about anything, after William had left with her. It was no big deal; he'd figured they'd call each other in the morning. But now he was nothing but glad she was there. He was warmed to the core. It was only in movies that someone threw pebbles at your window, though admittedly, his bedroom was on the first floor, and she could have just knocked. He wrapped his arms around her and led her inside. Luckily she didn't feel like talking. She crawled into bed beside him, and he went back to dreaming about spreading tar.

It was never discussed; she would have *loved* to discuss it: Why she'd gotten so irrational, why he hadn't gone after her instead of William, what would have happened if she *hadn't* gone over to his house, and so forth, but Roger wasn't the discussion type. She could never slow him down enough to talk about "life," those long cozy reminiscences of terrible times past: the terrible time she had won "Pin the Tail on the Donkey" after peeking under the blindfold, and the birthday girl as punishment for having already opened the prize had had to give up her favorite present to Lizzie, the guilt-ridden cheater!; the time she wet her pants in the first grade and had to walk around backwards; the long, ever-fascinating line of failed romances, etc. And when *finally* one Saturday afternoon she got Roger to lie down on the bed to listen to records, he'd listened to Bob Dylan moaning about one thing or another for a minute or two, said, "Gee, does this make me deep?"promptly noticed that she needed a table on her side of the bed and was gone lickety-split down into the basement to build her one, the electric saw whirring deafeningly in his ears, infusing a mindless peace in his soul that no drug could equal.

8

The Last Fight

One afternoon she abandoned the mess in her apartment and wandered down to the Harvard alumni office, where she saw a notice on the job board about paralegal work for the Department of Correction. The next thing she knew, to the horror of her liberal friends, she had a job in the legal department of the Department of Correction, working against prisoners.

At first she'd thought the job had something to do with correcting forms. She kept wondering why the guy who was interviewing her kept bringing up prisoners. She'd nodded pleasantly, humoring him. They'd gotten along great. She liked him, he didn't care that she couldn't type, even though the "paralegal job" was technically a "clerk-typist" job, civil service grade nine (what, she wondered, did a grade one do?); he just wanted to have someone smart whom he could teach how to draft pleadings. Smart, he actually used the word; it meant he had a sense of humor. People without a sense of humor always looked at her sadly and tried to buck up her confidence. Like when half her dress had gotten loaded with the paper in the Xerox machine, everyone at PRV had looked at her in that kind way, as if she'd just received her certification for Massachusetts Mental Hospital. She was smart in some ways, or anyway, she *used* to be smart. Now that she was grown-up it was hard to put your finger on what exactly these ways were.

When at the end of the interview he offered her the job, she accepted—just as she had accepted every job that had ever been offered her. She still couldn't believe that anyone would actually *pay* her to do anything. It was not until she got over to Roger's that night that it became clear what the Department of Correction really stood for. Her mother's theory on why she didn't notice such things was that she'd been so nearsighted as a little girl, a theory that was also supposed to explain why she'd clung to her mother's legs wherever she went. Lizzie suspected her clinging had a tiny bit more to do with the fact that her mother had been in the mental hospital the first two years of Lizzie's life. Anyway, at Roger's she learned what the Department of Correction was. All she could say in her defense was that when she was growing up, they had *reformed* prisoners, now they were *correcting* them. Was this a step up or a step down for the prisoner?

What would her job be? This took a little figuring out, since when the guy had been going on about prisoners she'd taken a little break and wondered how was she *ever* going to get her car inspected—how in the world *did* people who had jobs get their laundry done, let alone their cars inspected? At any rate, Roger and she figured her job would be helping the state deny prisoners their civil rights. Oh, this would be a big hit with her friends from PRV and college. Thank heavens Roger had none of the righteousness of the PRVers, most of whom had gone straight from the wombs of ivy colleges to the womb of PRV and didn't know anything about anything. Roger had a similar background, of course, but for some reason (was it that terrible tan leather jacket?) he seemed different. Besides, said Roger who knew lots of cons through his job, they're all as guilty as hell.

With Roger there were never any of those intense what-are-you-doing-with-your-life conversations she'd had with Tom Koch. Tom! She felt a little guilty about Tom; sometimes they had lunch together. After all, hadn't she been in love with him? Roger was the exact opposite— not an anguished conversation about anything. Just cook up some fresh vegetables from Roger's garden, drink some wine, go to bed. Plus he had a washer and dryer in his basement. She was having so much fun she felt guilty.

They danced in the living room to Tommy Snow records. Then they went out to celebrate her new job. They were always going out to celebrate.

He *hated* fighting—well, he couldn't even say that because he had never really fought with anyone. At home his parents had barely spoken to each other, let alone had words. Christ, the silences in the house after his brother, who was five years older, had gone off to boarding school. They weren't silences, exactly: He remembered with a shudder his mother chatting away cheerfully while his father turned the pages of the paper. Nobody had fought in his family, the golden opportunities of dinner-table indigestion carefully avoided by always eating supper on trays in front of the TV, usually while his father was still at the office. Dinnertime was watching "Superman" with your brother while your mother nursed her bourbon and water.

He didn't really see the point of fights and he certainly didn't see the point in discussing them after you had them. "I've never looked back in my life," he'd once told Lizzie, who'd asked, "Is this something you're proud of?"

There was one more incident a few weeks after Logan's party that came close to being a fight, and after that he won out, and they never fought again. It took place the night after he had gone with her to listen to Harry play with Van Morrison and in the process had met her parents. It had all been very convivial; he prided himself in being able to talk to people's parents because he was truly interested in different points of view, and he was always the one at the wedding who took the mother-in-law or Great-Aunt Tilly, or whoever needed to be gotten out of the way, over to the bar for a couple of stingers. Besides, her parents were very, very nice people; frankly he couldn't believe how normal they seemed, considering their children. At any rate, everything had been great. Then the next night she'd started talking about getting together that weekend with her cousin Art who was coming to town.

"Enough with the family," he'd said.

"What's that supposed to mean?" she said.

"I mean we just saw your family last night, how many goddamn nights in a row do we have to hang out with your family?" He could see he was making her mad; don't tell him they were going to have an honest-to-God argument. "I mean, Jesus, let's not have a fucking fight about it. Forget it. We'll see your family every fucking night of the week if you want, and twice on Sunday, let's just not fight about it, okay? Everything's been going great. I just want to play this thing out."

"Excuse me," she said slowly, "you want to *what*?"

"Play this thing out. Have a great time while it lasts. I mean, it's not like we're going to get married or something. I'm thirty-one years old, I've been out with a shit-load of girls, it's silly to think we're going to goddamn get married. I mean, what are the percentages we're likely to get married? One percent, three percent, no percent?"

"Well, I'm twenty-four and maybe I've slept with a few guys but I *never* sleep with anyone unless I think there's at least the chance, however distant—and I have to say with some it's been a bit on the distant side—anyway, there always has to be the *chance* we'll get married in the end. Otherwise, if there's no chance you're going to marry them, it's just awful."

"Give me a break. You've slept with a lot of jerks just the way I have. Guys you would never have married. It's the same thing. You just look at it differently, but it's the same thing." It killed him when people weren't rational. Why couldn't she, just once in her life, look at it rationally, look at *anything* rationally?

"Maybe it is," she huffed, "but it's just the way I am." Then they'd stopped talking about it—neither of them was particularly angry—and gone to bed. She read with the little light he'd rigged up so she could read all night and not wake him. Once she'd tried to read him Henry James on a car trip and he'd gotten so sleepy he'd swerved off the road. He read his three sentences of the latest Time-Life book, *Electrical Wiring*, and flipped off his light.

The thing was, he didn't want to make promises and hurt feelings. He'd vowed never to do any of that again after what he'd done to Nell Hafferoff. Nell Hafferoff was a tall, wispy brunette, the only skinny girl he'd ever made a play for.

She was a nice girl, a modern dance instructor, who lived in Cambridge, which made her kind of artsy, different than the girls he'd met at Brandy's after he'd broken up with Jenny Sands. Never had any of those women met his parents—except for the one who by a tragic twist of fate got taken out to a fancy dinner by his father and his stepmother, the time they'd decided to extend their visit an extra day. What else could he have done? He'd already made a date with this girl, a short blond with big breasts who liked to laugh and used to walk around the bedroom in curlers, so on she'd come to Au Beauchamps. Her sister was a topless dancer at a club; he had thought this was kind of cool, till he'd come back from the men's room that night and seen his father and the girl, all a titter, gabbing away, and suddenly he'd wondered if she could possibly have happened to mention her sister in the course of conversation.

But Nell Hafferoff was the kind of girl you could introduce to your parents. It was 1969, he'd been out of college a couple of years, and he'd gone out with her for several months—his goal was simply to get in her pants. She was a pleasant girl, which was why he was inclined to go out with her so long without getting anything; she was very straight, virginal, he thought maybe she was Catholic. The problem was, she could put you to sleep in about four sentences. She had this sweet, soft voice, and one time on a double date with his friend Rick, they were having drinks and he kept turning to Rick and saying, under his breath, "What am I going to do? She bores me to fucking tears," and then he'd turn back to Nell who was talking soporifically away, and space out completely, trying to prop his eyes open by changing positions in his chair and interjecting an uh-huh, yep, no kidding, or laughing at proper rhythmic intervals, wondering Is this really worth it just to get into her pants? when suddenly he'd noticed she'd stopped talking and was sitting there looking at him expectantly, waiting for an answer. He smiled at her encouragingly, hoping against hope that maybe she'd paused for breath, or maybe it was a pause for emphasis.

"Well," she said, "what do *you* think?"

"Well, Nell," he'd said, "that's an interesting question, a *very* interesting question. Uh, excuse me for *one* second, I've just got to ask my friend Rick this one important thing, very important—Rick? Tell me, what do you think about Havlicek scoring forty-eight points?"

At any rate, after several months he'd slowly progressed to a little second base. (What, was he still in high school?) This he'd been granted the night when, after several Budweisers, he'd fashioned an angel for the top of Nell's Christmas tree out of a beercan and tin foil—oh, that angel was a big thing, she'd shown everybody that angel. And then one night soon after while they were making out at her apartment, he'd said, "Jeez, I think I'm falling for you," and Boom! the panties were off. Afterwards all he'd wanted was to get out of there; he couldn't even bring himself to spend the night.

He'd told a dozen other women he loved them, and never had a second thought. And yet this time, he was frightened, frightened to talk to her after what he'd done. Weeks went by, and then finally she called. He was in the kitchen and the phone rang and he hadn't called her since the night he'd gotten into her pants and he grabbed the phone and got that breathy little "Hi Roger, it's Nell."

"Hi!! Jesus, you got me right in the middle of something, can I call you *right* back?"

"Sure," said Nell. And he *never* called her back.

Later he heard how she'd been devastated, quit her job, and moved to some place like Greece. He still felt it was the worst thing he had ever done. He'd lied to women before but he had always said something at the end to at least let them know the relationship was over. Even when he was twelve and would dance for hours on end, arms wrapped around Buffy Philbrick—too terrified to kiss her—even with Buffy Philbrick, he had had the consideration to call her up. "Buffy," he'd said huskily over the phone, "I just, well, I think we should break up."

"But why?" Buffy had asked.

"Well, it's just that, well; Buffy, I'd rather be single."

At any rate, he would go to his grave feeling bad about what he'd done to Nell Hafferoff, and he never wanted to make any promises to anyone or hurt anyone's feelings ever again.

When he woke up the next morning and looked at Lizzie, lying there with her ridiculous hair, he realized it was no use. He loved her.

9

Roger Ponders

He didn't propose to her until eight months later. Even after the proposal, sometimes he'd look at her with her brown hair, black tights, and Chinese shoes and think: I can't believe this is the girl I am going to marry. He'd always envisioned the girl he would marry walking down the street in high heels with big breasts and blond hair flowing down her back. Lizzie looked like something out of Dickens, not that he'd ever read Dickens, not since his days at Exeter when he'd come back exhausted from playing hockey all afternoon and have to jam his eyes open to read about "Pip" and some pie in the larder.

He must have gotten the idea from the time his mother visited and called her Little Dorrit. She'd been wearing barrettes that day, denting her hair on either side of her part into two explosions of fuzz, and a long maroon flannel skirt and ballet slippers, which she scampered all over the ground with, although it must have been near freezing. He watched her (stone sober) walking gaily along in the tall grasses in the field across from Brookhill, the mental hospital—she said she *loved* to pic-

nic across from Brookhill because her brothers had
"graduated" from there, and it gave her a cozy feeling
(Jesus!)—singing "I'm going to a huke lah . . . a huke
huke huke huke laaa" softly to no one in particular, and
he would think, I cannot believe this girl is the one. But
when he looked at her he loved her so much that it hurt.

He'd never even known anyone who had been to a
psychiatrist, and now he was thinking of marrying a girl
who only felt cozy picnicking next to a mental hospital!
A girl who'd spent her teens watching various members
of her family play athletics at the local loony bin. "What
about Spencer?" he had said hopefully one day. "*He's
not crazy?*" Even as he spoke, though, he was getting this
sinking feeling remembering Spencer one winter afternoon skating all by himself back and forth across Spy
Pond, dribbling a hockey puck as if he were center for
the Boston Bruins and it was the play-offs (while Lizzie
had been off on the other side of the pond skating happily away waving a large branch). "Well," Lizzie had
mused, "there *are* some who consider him crazier than
Harry. Dr. Trumbull says—" He didn't want to know. He
guessed that Lizzie herself had been to any number of
shrinks. In his family no one ever admitted to having had
a bad day, let alone went and spent money to talk to
some perfect stranger about it. Roger considered bad
days a challenge, something to turn around. When things
piled up in a day and ended with his car being towed, he
would say, "I won't allow this to be a bad day," smoke a
joint, and go out to a bar to have some laughs. When
he'd hit thirty and this attitude no longer worked 100
percent of the time, he had progressed to saying to himself, "Okay, this is a bad day. I'm just going to chalk it
off to a bad day," and gone to bed at 8:30, straight to
sleep, and when he woke up he always felt better.

He just didn't understand people who let themselves

be depressed, and wanted to say to them just what his mother had always said (his mother who chopped her own wood at sixty and spoke rousingly of the hardships of the depression, even though as a child she'd been driven around by a chauffeur on Halloween): "Pull yourself up by your bootstraps." If you couldn't pull yourself up by your bootstraps, what was the point? Still, he wasn't so brazenly intolerant as he'd been in his straight and narrow days, when at age twenty-one, walking down a city street with his usual swagger, he'd been stopped by a young black kid panhandling and had launched into a long lecture, the gist of it being: "Wouldn't you feel better if you went out and got a job and earned the dollars yourself?" When he'd finally finished, the kid had looked at him with a frightened face and said, "Gee, are you a cop?"

He'd never actually considered the word "marriage" in connection with Lizzie until one Saturday in July (they'd been going out almost a year), when he was driving off to the Lumber Barn. It was the first time he had thought about marriage with someone since the early days with Jenny Sands. Now he had to ask himself why he hadn't married Jenny Sands. How had he managed to be in love with Jenny Sands for four years and never marry her? And yet he knew if he had married Jenny Sands, he would be divorced by now, probably with a couple of kids. She would have wanted kids right away; Christ, she was studying to be a *kindergarten* teacher, and if that wasn't a sign of things to come, what was? He was afraid of commitment, Jenny had said—well, it didn't take an Einstein to figure that out. Who wouldn't be afraid of commitment? He'd never seen anyone happily committed to anyone; he could only assume any marriage for him would be a disaster.

All right, so a lot of people don't marry their first true

love. But then you get into your thirties and you still haven't met someone yet, and you keep thinking, When is it going to happen? Would it ever happen? Maybe there was something screwed up in him where he couldn't fall in love with anyone—maybe Jenny was it. Then, of course, this immediately got converted into a great line to use to break up with someone, and even worse, a great line to get someone in the sack. "You know," he'd explain at the end of an evening, "I just want to warn you, I can't seem to fall in love ... " Bingo, they'd be in bed in two minutes. Women loved the challenge; with them they knew it would be different. The problem was later, after they'd fallen in love with you (that was the other thing, they were *always* falling in love) and you were ready to be out of there and reminded them of that little initial conversation on the subject, they'd get mad as hornets.

At any rate, he asked himself, why was he thirty-one, almost thirty-two, and still not married? A few months before he'd met Lizzie he'd told John, his roommate, that eventually he thought he should be getting his own place—you know what people said about men living together after they turned thirty, ha, ha. Truth was, he was scared of living alone. The only way he knew to be alone was to stay active; if he didn't feel like working or doing a project, he went out on the town to be with people, once hitting eleven bars in a single night.

Then of course he'd met Lizzie, and it had all just moved along, no time to catch your breath. When they'd realized they were in love, things could hardly get any more romantic, because they'd always been so romantic, right from the very first day. She was twenty-four and like a little kid compared to the cynical girls he'd gotten used to, and he'd bought her all kinds of tacky gifts in Bermuda, and they'd had their picture taken in front of the towel with the fluorescent couple and the sunset that said "Together in Bermuda."

But he hadn't really gotten into trouble until that winter, when, sitting around a table of friends, had come blustering from his mouth one of his typical bravado statements: "I'm thirty-one years old and I've never lived with a girl in my life." What the point of this brag was, God knew. Lizzie had listened and then said, quietly, "What exactly is it that *we're* doing?" and of course it was true, they had been together every night since the first night, while she was paying rent on an apartment she hadn't been in for five months. Then the next day, Sunday, they'd gone out to a hip restaurant on St. Botolph's Street and had a conversation about how someday they should move to New York and live in a loft, the unspoken assumption being they would live in a loft *together*, and then a few days later he suggested she might just as well give up her apartment. The next time William had come over, he'd waltzed into Roger's bedroom to play a little tune on the piano Roger kept in the alcove, where instead he found himself standing with his hands poised over Lizzie's bureau. "Huh," he had remarked.

Their shacking up was no big deal to Lizzie's seasoned parents, who had been catapulted into the Age of Aquarius by screwed-up kids so eager to share with them their every flicker of negative emotion—a little healthy repression in that family sure would have gone a long way. He did, however, seem to remember the Reades over at the Watertown house for dinner one night and Mr. Reade looking around, asking casually, in honest perplexity, "So, where's Lizzie's room?"

For *his* mother, though, the living in sin was a big thing. He didn't think his mother had much of an idea of what his life was really like; his older brother was a mother's dream, worked for a Waspy law firm, had been married since his early twenties to a beautiful Southern girl who rented rug machines at night to keep her wall-to-wall carpeting pristine. He remembered when David and Audrey were first married visiting their tiny perfect apartment and getting yelled at for not folding the mono-grammed towels after he'd showered. Audrey was very exact, and he knew it drove her wild when she'd ask when he'd be getting there Thanksgiving day, and he'd say, don't worry about me, I'll be there when I'm there, just go ahead and eat without me. His mother greatly admired Audrey for being all the things a woman should be. In spite of his mother's constant fevered pitch of activity, her house was always hopelessly cluttered—you'd glance over at an armchair in the living room and there'd be a stack of Christmas cards from 1946 that she'd just happened to be perusing the night before. She couldn't bear to throw anything away; Baggies were hung to dry and her ex-husband's prescription drugs still in the cabinet from thirty years ago. "I can't tell you what that girl has done for that boy," she'd say of her daughter-in-law, as if the clean carpets and neat little lists on the refrigerator had dragged his brother up from the gutter to be partner in a fancy New York law firm.

Of course, it was no great mystery why his mother didn't know what Roger was really about; he never even wore his usual clothes around her, wearing instead the Brooks Brothers' outfits she inevitably gave him for Christmas. (Although he *had* drawn the line at wearing those pajamas like his father's with pullstrings. "It's none of my business," she'd called out one day from the laundry room, "but I strongly suspect you are wearing your underwear to bed.") Not that it had ever really occurred to him that he never wore jeans around his mother until Lizzie had brought it up. It had just been instinctive in him to wear what he'd been given to be polite, to avoid hurt feelings.

To his mother he had written a long, careful letter about how he and Lizzie had decided to live together, after hours of pondering (the idea of Lizzie and he pondering anything!), receiving in return a reply in which she said she dearly loved him but did not think he understood the meaning of the word commitment. Then came a quote, which actually he really liked, about how love made you real, from a sermon she had recently heard. As a child he'd never gone to Sunday school; he and his cousins had thrown firecrackers on Sunday mornings while their parents drank Bloody Marys. But after the divorce his mother had found religion in a big way, and now there were little penciled religious quotes all over the house: "Do unto others as you would have them do unto you" alongside of a note that said, "Please close the refrigerator door firmly, it bounces back." In the midst of all the cacophony, his favorite had said, "A whisper is worth a thousand words," written by his mother who had never lowered her voice in her life.

The quote she sent him in the letter was originally from a children's book, *The Velveteen Rabbit*, a copy of which his mother had enclosed. Lizzie had cried like a baby when she'd read it one Saturday afternoon lying in bed while he'd put up the storm windows.

He was on his way to the Lumber Barn that hot afternoon when he was pondering marriage with Lizzie, to buy insulation for the cabin on a lake in Maine he and Lizzie had bought in May. They'd purchased the place to use on weekends because he was always looking for projects. When you built something—whether it was the wooden drink-holders he'd personally designed for the dash of his car, staining it "walnut" and then protecting it with polyurethane, or the low bookcase he'd fashioned around three sides of his bed, the perfect place for his *Penthouse* magazines (well, it *had* been perfect, until Lizzie had arrived on the scene and begun kicking them off in her sleep)—beginning on a Saturday morning and finishing up around seven on a Sunday night, it gave you a wonderful sense of accomplishment. His life was predicated on how much he could accomplish in one day—it had been ingrained in him by his mother who, though she'd never earned a penny, worked all day from morning to nightfall, as if she had two jobs. Back from weeding the flowers in the center of town, or running the Bloodmobile, or scraping down the old paint in the pantry, when she lay down on the Madame Récamier couch in her drawing room at the end of the day, she literally was out of breath.

And then, of course, they needed a place for Hope and Leslie to run around. Actually, they'd gotten Hope and Leslie *after* they'd bought the cabin. Lizzie had been dying for a dog from the word go. "It's not fair to have a dog with both of us working all day," Roger, the voice of reason, had said, and then she'd countered with, "What if the dog was going to be gassed otherwise?" Not that he'd really been averse to having a dog—he'd always wanted one when he was young, but his mother had said she knew who would be walking and feeding that dog. Of course she was absolutely right. His mother had done everything around the house, from shoveling the front walk to making all the beds. He'd never lifted a finger. Lizzie always said she didn't understand why her brothers, who had been brought up doing carefully prescribed chores, as adults never helped around the house, whereas Roger couldn't stop. Of course, it was he who, when they went out to the pound, had said, why not take both, there were only two left of the "mixed retrievers" (the accent on "mixed") in the litter, both females, and he couldn't bear the thought of one being gassed. How could they take one and not the other? Lizzie couldn't have agreed more. He'd built "the girls" a pen that quickly became filled with little black dots. Whenever Hope or Leslie went to the bathroom Lizzie would call from the window "Good girls!!"—she said she wanted to try positive reinforcement on them as experiment for bringing up kids—with the result that, whenever Hope and Leslie went to the bathroom for the rest of their lives, he supposed, they would be looking up expectantly into the heavens, waiting for God's approbation.

At any rate, he and Lizzie had never even used the word "marriage" in ordinary conversation. He'd shielded himself from thinking about it, in spite of buying property and dogs with this woman—her name wasn't even on the deed, he had just taken her five thousand dollars without so much as a signature. But how could any of it be wrong? He couldn't imagine ever being without her. And yet he had never allowed this idea to translate into marriage until that afternoon on his way to the Lumber Barn.

He took a little break from thinking about discussing marriage with Lizzie in order to figure out how much insulation he was going to need to buy, what the square footage was, and what kind of nails to use. Insulating not only gave you a great sense of accomplishment, just thinking about it made you warm and tingly—after all you were literally warming the shelter where you were going to live. He'd always had quite a nesting instinct for a guy who'd never wanted to settle down.

He arrived at the Lumber Barn and had a long discussion with Lenny. They decided on roofing nails because they were long enough to get through the layers and had fat heads. He was very proud of the way he was doing the ceiling, stuffing six inches of fiberglass between the rafters and then getting tongue-and-groove rigid-board Styrofoam to fit over. Lizzie maintained that when friends casually asked what he was doing with the ceiling, they didn't really want to know all the sordid details, they were just being polite, but he disagreed. It was really very interesting, although sometimes he supposed he got a little carried away in the length of its description. He loved that ceiling. A cushy job compared to lying under the house and stuffing fiberglass in under the floor, spitting pieces of it out of your mouth. The dogs loved to crawl under the house where he'd stuffed it; Lizzie called it the cancer ward and worried Leslie was addicted. The only thing that drew Leslie away was the sound above of Lizzie and Roger pulling up chairs to eat. Yes, he certainly was having such a great time with Lizzie. He figured, if they got married it would just be double the fun. Double the fun—that really was the way to look at it.

10

Lizzie Ponders

It sure was a good thing her social life was going so well, because no one, and she meant no one, could ever accuse her of letting her work interfere with her life. This is what she did at her job: nothing. This was not an exaggeration. Ever since she'd been promoted to "Assistant Program Development Specialist," a grade fourteen, quite a leap (Roger had been so proud: "You're on your way!" he'd said, tears welling in his eyes, although neither he nor anyone else for that matter had a clue in heaven what an Assistant Program Development Specialist *was*)—ever since she'd moved down the hall to don the mantle of this illustrious position, she'd had not a letter to write, not a memo to read, not even a desk to tidy up, because there was not one single thing on it. She even had a secretary, who hated her because there had been quite some feeling in the single-digited ranks of the department that this secretary should have automatically advanced to the Assistant Program Development Specialist opening, even though, as Lizzie's new boss had explained gently to the girl, she didn't have the skills for the job.

(The skills for the job! thought Lizzie, pinching herself awake). This was the mentality of working for the state: No one ever got fired and the next person in line got the job. She'd learned this back in the good old days a few months before when she was just a grade nine, back when she'd been busy as a beaver, drafting and typing (with a self-correcting typewriter) pleading after pleading.

It all had been a whirl in that legal department— things had yet to simmer down from the sixties when people like Mr. Bacon (who had married the Texaco heiress) had gone as observers to the prisons, and, as a result, every Tom, Dick, and Harry in the can was writing himself a legal brief and suing the state. Boy, these guys were tough, not exactly what you had in mind when you dreamed of rehabilitating prisoners with Shakespeare's sonnets. She was less shocked than she'd expected when one of the prison superintendents (one night she'd gone out to dinner with all of them—hardly what she'd imagined herself doing her second year out of college) told her he was actually *in favor* of the death penalty; in fact, she almost saw his point. She who had trounced captial punishment, and, more importantly, that bossy Belle Hallenkemp, in the fifth-grade debate on the subject! At any rate, the lawyers in the department had been so busy that they had her pretend she was a lawyer and sent her to attend the interminable union meetings. "Don't worry," they said, "nobody will ask you anything. Just scribble notes now and then and look stern." She used to get all sorts of important-looking packets addressed to her as "Esquire," documents that were completely incomprehensible, though beautifully typed: page after page of section this, bylaw that, that went straight from her hands into the wastebasket, the lawyers refusing even to spare them a glance.

Then of course there'd been the little excitement of the

bomb scare. She was typing away one afternoon when the phone rang. "Department of Correction," she'd answered in a crisp voice.

"There's a bomb going off in ten minutes," the caller had graciously informed her and then hung up. With remarkable presence of mind she'd quietly walked into her boss's office and said in a lowered voice, "Get your coats, we're getting out of here: There's a bomb going off in ten minutes."

"Elizabeth," her boss had said, "do you think we might share this with the others?"

Of all the hundreds and hundreds of drones working for the state in the Cabot Chittenden building, somehow it would have been she who would have received the bomb threat that emptied the entire building. Cabot Chittenden was her cousin, of course—first cousin twice removed, or something—though she hadn't known he'd had a building named after him until the day of her interview when she'd gotten out of the taxi and looked up at the name embossed on the thirty-storied building. "Well, I'll be," she'd said, "Cousin Chit!" then walked into the lobby where the man with no legs sold candy bars. She had always wondered where all the people she saw on the subway were when they weren't on the subway, with their faces staring hopelessly before them; it turned out they worked for the state. It still made her want to cry every morning to see them coming in droves to buy lottery tickets, especially when she thought of her "patrician" Cousin Chit, trust funds coming out his ears, having high tea on the terrace of his estate in Wellesley. Real life was the worst thing in the world; it was one reason she never read the papers. Whenever she happened to take a glance at the front page, she would rush to Roger in a panic saying, "the world's going to end, just look at this!", and he, who spent his life's blood trying to move people with the reality of world events, would say, "Lizzie, the answer to you and current events is just don't read the papers."

But now, here she sat, no phones to answer, oh no, her time now was too valuable for that, trying to make it through minute after minute of excruciating boredom. She shared the office with her boss, a really cute black guy, enormously successful, but, come to think of it, what *did* he do? She couldn't really figure it out, but he managed to always be bustling about and clapping people on the back. She had to fake being occupied and looked with longing at all the papers on his desk. Couldn't he share them with her, give her something to shuffle around, she wondered, feeling a covetousness welling up inside her. Still she was too paralyzed by boredom to ask him for something to do; plus, when she'd made the mistake of asking what could she do the first day, he'd said, "How about the files? The files always need some help." The files! She'd spent a couple of hours opening and closing the cabinets, looking at the names on the folders, wondering what on earth he could have had in mind for them.

Sometimes she didn't know if she could stand it till Friday. Friday was the day, she was proud to say, that the prisons (five in all) called in with their body counts. "Why, you can take the prison count!" her boss had called out finally one day, a stroke of genius, no wonder this guy was going places! She always came in her most official costume on Fridays and rustled about getting her desk ready for the big moment. After she received the prison counts she added them up on the calculator twice, then did it longhand.

This was the extent of her career in the spring of 1976. She was making two hundred dollars a week—the same salary level as a correctional guard—and it was the most she had ever made. But she didn't know how long she could stick it out. She was so happy otherwise; she knew it wasn't supposed to be true, but she couldn't help thinking that she could never be ambitious careerwise and in love at the same time. There had been that brief time in college when she was burning, burning, burning! to be a writer—she had had this vision of herself sitting by a window writing lyrically away through the sunny afternoons of her life, her hair tied back in a ribbon— and for three weeks there had not been a man on her mind until she'd felt so strong and proud that she'd swept the trumpet player from Harry's band right off his feet, and then, try as she might (half the reason he liked her had been this so-called novel she'd been writing), not another decent word ever made it to the page.

"I wish I could be a writer," she would say to Roger, "but I can't write because I'm not depressed enough." This drove Roger crazy. But of course she was right—all she had to do was look around. Cousin Charlie, Pulitzer Prize, crazy as a loon. Harry, brilliant musician, three breakdowns. All her life a connection between genius, misery, and insanity had been implied. Being a genius meant that people in the family would let you finish a sentence (just once!) and speak about you in reverential tones. For years she'd grappled with the question of whether to be a genius and not be expected to unload the dishwasher, on the good side, but on the bad side have to check in at the mental hospital on a regular basis, until finally it had dawned on her you didn't actually *have* to make the momentous decision on *whether* to be a genius or not if you *weren't* a genius.

Roger, of course, was completely different from the people she had known. Roger never agonized about any-thing; he was too busy succeeding. "Frankly," he said, "depression is a bore." Roger was always very frank, although sometimes he was merely quite honest. "Quite honestly," he'd said in a loud voice one night just as the restaurant hit a lull, "I *always* wear pajama bottoms." They'd been discussing bathrobes and getting quite animated. Roger thought psychiatry was a crutch. One passing reference to poor old Ms. Greenette, the social worker ("You're seeing a *what*?"), and she was history. No, Roger was never depressed, and, the great thing was, neither was Lizzie, now that she was with him. Everything was great, all the time, everything was fun, whether it was buying corn or buying four acres on a lake in Maine.

Four acres on a lake in Maine, how had it happened? Her parents had carefully waited until they were over fifty before buying their second house, on a mere half acre. With her parents everything was planned; they hadn't bought the place until the brothers were through college, or rather through with college, dropping out early on, and then, of course, they'd bought something simple with no mortgage. But for Roger and Lizzie the thought became the deed within seconds. He'd mentioned how he'd always wanted to look for some land in Maine and she'd mentioned this $5,000 inheritance she was getting in March, a check that barely graced her hand before flying off endorsed to Roger to the bank to await clearing.

Roger and she had been looking for a farm for about thirty thousand, but when they saw this land on a lake for sixty, well, they just *had* to have it, even with an enormous mortgage. It was that simple. There was this sort of vague theory of subdividing later, quickly forgotten. Where did Roger get such confidence, she wondered, and then she saw where, when his father showed up and offered to hold the mortgage, interest free. She'd kept nodding meaningfully at Roger over his father's head, but he'd ignored her, and refused the offer, explaining that he only wanted to borrow money at a fair interest.

Her thug boyfriend, she called him, in that he said "irregardless" and "by the same token" and wore perfectly awful synthetic body shirts that had girls' faces peeking from behind trees. She'd been so proud of liking someone from a different background! It took her a couple of weeks to factor in that Roger came from Greenwich, Connecticut, and had gone to prep school.

So here she was, living on Roger's bandwagon, she who had always fallen for the whiners and the mopers! Of course, she probably would have jumped on anyone's bandwagon that drunken night at William's party, but by sheer dumb luck, she had ended up on Roger's. Now she was living on a plane she had longingly seen others on, where you woke up in the morning and did things like go to the cleaners in a happy, normal, whistling way, instead of passing the cleaners every single day weighed down by guilt about the three skirts you'd left off on a one-day special six months before.

Now she was normal, better than normal; now it was *fun* to go to the grocery store. She was in love, in love with someone who led a charmed life. And, he was in love with her!

So things were going along great, although at the moment she was up in the cabin in Maine worrying about how to explain the fact of her and Roger's living in sin to Great-Aunt Elizabeth and Great-Uncle Win, who were coming up the next day to look at the graves in the old Chittenden cemetery in Camden for the hundred and fifth time, then turn right around and drive home again. Her mother had once called her up at 7:30 A.M. to ask her if she wanted to be buried in the cemetery in Camden, as they were running out of room. She was on her way to the bathroom thinking about what utter lie to come up with, when with a loud snap the hanger Roger had rigged up to keep shut the bathroom door (now a foot wide with insulation) suddenly attacked her in the eye, whacking her contact lens right out to God knew where. *Of course* she didn't have a spare pair; she knew Roger would ask her if she had a spare pair. She hadn't been able to locate the insurance form the last time she'd lost a contact lens (and then the other lens immediately thereafter), so she'd just naturally gone straight to the spare pair, with a vague resolution to keep looking for that insurance form.

She was absolutely *furious* at Roger for putting that hanger up there on the door. He should have known better!

11

Lizzie Is Persuaded

"Okay," Roger said to himself as he turned the Peugeot into the dirt driveway of the cabin, "we're going to at least *discuss* the marriage question." The word still stuck in his throat, but, he supposed, the time had come to start thinking about it. He got out of the car, shut the door, and took a deep breath. Yes, he certainly loved Lizzie, no doubt about that; life had certainly picked up since Lizzie. Double the fun, he said to himself again as he opened the door to the cabin.

She was on all fours on the kitchen floor looking for something. He could tell by the way she moved that she was mad at him. "It's my contacts," she cried out. "That *hanger* you were so proud of whacked me in the eye." "Don't you have a spare pair?" he asked. He helped her look for a while, until she said, forget it, it was hopeless—now she would get a headache and have to go around squinting for a week.

Maybe this wasn't the time, he thought hopefully. Finally, though, she calmed down. They were sitting on the green corduroy couch with the white stain where she'd poured an entire bucket of bleach after removing a dead mouse. He plowed ahead.

"You know, Lizzie," he said, though he was already not enjoying this, "it's just that, well, we've never really discussed marriage. I mean, what do you think?"

"Well," she said, brightening up about one hundred watts, "I think it's great!"

"Oh!" he said. Where were all those things to be considered? He couldn't remember a blessed one. "Do you think we should get married?" Jesus! What was he saying? Why hadn't he lowered his voice at the end of the sentence or something to make it more rhetorical?

"Yeah!" she said. She was goddamn bursting with happiness.

"Oh!" he said, "Great!" and then there were all kinds of hugs and kisses and let's-go-out-and-celebrates, and all he could think was, Whoa Nelly . . . hold your horses! This is going too fast—all he'd wanted to do was *discuss* the idea. Weren't you supposed to discuss these things that were going to affect the rest of your life? She'd always wanted to discuss things, all the times before, ad nauseam; where was all this talking-matters-over now? He had wanted the kind of careful conversation he might have had with Jenny Sands, with yes, let's get married, but certainly not *now*, absolutely out of the question to get married *now*. He remembered the night—he must have been a junior—when he and Jenny had gone around a party shyly telling everyone they were going to get married someday. *Someday*—that was the word he was looking for! We think we should get married *someday*. But what could he do, everything always went at breakneck speed with Lizzie and him. It was too late.

They'd wanted to go to the Cranberry Hill Inn, but they wouldn't let Roger in because he didn't have a jacket, and they'd found themselves at Long John's Tavern, a ye olde bluff kind of place that didn't have a single thing they ordered left on the menu. So they ended with cheese and crackers on a paddleboard for their engagement celebration. But she didn't care, she was so happy! She had been waiting and waiting for Roger to propose; she would have never dared to bring it up. No one would have dared. ("So when are you getting married?" William had kept asking her, but never ever Roger.) But when he finally proposed, she hadn't been surprised; she knew he loved her.

Still, she would have preferred a touch more joviality to mark the occasion. Generally, Roger used the merest occasion as a reason to order up a lot of drinks. But now he sat nursing a bottle of beer, a queasy smile affixed to his face, barely speaking. However, she was prepared to overlook this. She was so happy. She was getting married!

It took a day for it to dawn on her, then it did.

"You don't want to marry me!" she said out of the blue, or so it seemed to Roger. It was the next afternoon, and they were lying on the raft, which he had finished building (by flashlight in the dark) the night before. He had used the planks off one of the outhouses at the camp, carefully pulling down the building the day before, saving most of the nails.

"Of course I want to marry you," he said.

"No, you *don't!*" she said, sobbing now. She had a point, of course, Roger had to admit, but as he lay watching her shuddering body, he felt something deep in his gut. To his surprise, he *did* want to marry her!

"I do want to marry you," he said.

"You do *not*," she cried, crawling to the furthest corner of the raft.

"I do! Please marry me, Lizzie," he said, "please, *please*!" He was practically crying too. He couldn't *stand* to see her so unhappy. "No, no, no," she said, keeping her face away from him and weeping into the lake, "I'll never marry you, not in a million years."

"Please, Lizzie!! Please!!" he would have been on his knees if he hadn't started lying down. "*Please* marry me!"

"Well," she sniffled, "all *right*."

12

Roger Has a Drink

Put the questions out of your mind, place one foot in front of the other, and go forward. But he wasn't being stoic; he felt great.

Suddenly there was no man on earth more excited to be getting married than Roger Stoner. It was *he* who insisted on springing the news on Lizzie's parents the next day over lavish servings of Chicken Divan, a dish for twelve prepared for the coming to New Hampshire of Great-Aunt Elizabeth and Great-Uncle Win, who had simply never shown up.

"So," Roger had said over an enormous plate of food, "we're getting married!" Both the parents had started to cry.

"I sort of thought of you as already married," Mr. Reade had sniffled.

"We've *got* to book the Country Club!" Mrs. Reade had cried, grabbing a pencil to begin a list. Roger called his parents. They called Lizzie's brothers; he called his own brother. They called everyone.

He even loved meeting with the minister, Roger who had never had one serious thought about God, except in

a mad-dash sort of way, he, Roger Stoner, had sat in the
minister's office chatting merrily about life and the meaning of commitment, as relaxed as if he were in the midst
of a profound discussion with William over which bar to
try next. Lizzie had looked at him aghast, dumbstruck,
though later making the remark that Roger had particularly perked up when the reverend had begun discussing
annulment. Not true, he averred, he'd loved all of it
equally, the whole thing, every minute of it. He supposed
it was because it was all so safe—how dangerous could it
get, with the minister sitting right there? He loved the
minister—a real lefty, who'd been the curate when Lizzie
had been confirmed at the Episcopal church in Concord,
a guy who'd marched in Birmingham, appearing, to the
discomfort of the half of Trinity Church who did not car-
pool into Roxbury Wednesday mornings to paint poor
people's walls, on the front page of the *Concord Journal*
in 1964, his arms flung enthusiastically round several
black people. He almost embraced the minister when he
suggested Roger have his mother give *him* away, an idea
that died quickly when reported to his mother, who had
almost left the church when they started making everyone turn and hug the stranger next to them.

He loved the idea of the wedding. He began producing it in his mind. He and Lizzie both loved being the
center of attention; it would be a great party. Lizzie and
he looping around the dance floor showing off, just as
they did for company in Maine, swinging each other,
between shots of tequila, around a tree off a twenty-foot
precipice, at two in the morning. His family, all decked
out, looking in their tall Waspy way indistinguishable
from the Reades, everyone good-looking, everyone blitzed.
The Reade brothers, crazy as loons, but nobody said they
weren't talented, playing Dixieland music, George on
piano, Spencer singing "You're a sweetheart" in his pure

voice, Harry gigantic on sax and clarinet. Mr. Reade on banjo, with a smile, still teary-eyed from walking his only daughter down the aisle, though knowing Lizzie, who for starters would probably cut herself shaving her legs and arrive at the church sheathed in Band-Aids, would have raced him down the aisle. She always walked too fast, she said it was from trying to keep up with Harry all her life.

Even the leaves would be at their October brightest. It would be sunny; Roger always took it personally if it was cloudy on a weekend. Lizzie said if she were God, she would just say to hell with it and make it sunny every weekend, anything to avoid crossing Roger Stoner when it came to having a good time. After a couple of scotches, he'd sit in on drums, while his father, who loved Dixieland, would stand nearby. "Have you ever had so much fun in your life?" Roger would ask and his father would answer in his understated way, "Just right, Rog." You could make a case that his father would be the happiest of everyone—that his son wasn't marrying the blond whose sister danced topless, that he was getting married at all.

His father absolutely adored Lizzie. For one thing she could play poker. One of the few times Roger had ever heard disappointment in his father's voice was when Lizzie had called him up and put Roger on the phone to be told that aces over deuces beat kings over queens. "Oh, Roger," his father had sighed with a poignance absent even the night Roger had called him from jail asking for bail money. Sometimes Lizzie would tell the other players exactly what she had in her hand, then clean up because nobody had believed her. Roger himself was a terrible card player—he hated card games because there was no energy being expended—and a worse sport. He, the big hockey hero, would leave in the middle of a hand if he was losing. Anyway, his father loved Lizzie, her out-rageousness. He was very introverted, or so Roger had been told, except when he was around Roger, and now around Lizzie his father lit up. His father, he had just begun to realize, was pretty sappy, and actually sent Lizzie a baby picture of Roger (straight from the womb and looking ready to party) signed *From your future husband*. It gave Roger a shudder; his father'd been anything but sentimental with his mother.

His mother would be at the opposite side of the reception from his father (and, of course, Mrs. Ash), drinking a bourbon and telling stories in her gravelly voice and probably wearing that old straw hat with flowers that she always said ought to have two holes in it for the donkey ears. His mother liked Lizzie, although he was sure she wondered just what kind of a housewife she would make. "Waste not, want not," she'd said more than once to Lizzie who couldn't for the life of her grab a paper towel to pick up a tiny spill without dragging along half the roll with it.

He was getting married! And he had not a single worry in the world through it all—except for one ten-minute period on the morning of the wedding. Lizzie had slept at her parents', but he'd had a houseful at the Watertown house that night and for breakfast the next morning, and then he'd driven over to the Colonial Inn in Concord to get dressed in his morning coat at his brother's room. It was his wedding day after all, weren't you supposed to do stuff like that on your wedding day? He was looking forward to it. He liked his shy, older brother; not that they had a lot in common, his brother who went to paddle tennis suppers with his wife at the club. But when he arrived at the inn, David wasn't there, just a note about how he had to get a tire fixed for the ride home that evening.

Suddenly he was terribly lonely—he got that pit in his stomach like the one he got the time he'd passed a Brigham's and happened to glance in and see a man eating a sandwich by himself; the man had looked perfectly content, but for some reason the scene had frightened Roger to death. His biggest fear was of being alone—his entire single life he had always been sure to have projects to occupy him until (well, he was the first one to admit it) the next drink.

He stood in David's hotel room. He had one hour in which to get dressed, and he figured it would take him approximately one minute, max. He wished he hadn't already shaved and showered. He always shaved in the shower to save time. Lizzie, who was constantly worriedly catching her reflection in toasters and shop windows, said she couldn't believe that he could go through a whole day without once looking in the mirror. Well, he'd saved all that valuable time this morning and now he was in a hotel room all by himself with absolutely nothing to do. There were no projects in a hotel room, no legs to be sawed off tables or windows to caulk, and it was only 11:00 in the morning—he couldn't drink alone in the bar at that hour, it was worse than the guy at Brigham's. All of a sudden on this great, happy day, he was left to himself. He'd counted on David to fill this hour, to have a little talk along the lines of "So this is quite a day, getting married and all . . . " or, "So . . . you're married, huh?" Nothing deeper than that; God knew, he didn't want to unduly alarm anyone in his family by getting deep. The only time in his life he had ever discussed anything personal with his mother was after his parents had announced they were getting divorced, and Jenny Sands had made him ask his mother how she felt. There had been a few awkward exchanges, and then his mother had said, "And we'll never talk about this again." And they never had.

Actually, the truth was, he didn't really care about talking to his brother about life, even in the most superficial way; he'd just needed him to fill the gap, the gap between 11:00 and 12:00 when he'd be surrounded again by people. So where was David? The room was stifling; he was having a hard time catching his breath. He picked up a chair—what did he think he was going to do, dash it against the antique glass window? Then suddenly he remembered. His mother was there. And Aunt Cornelia. That meant Bloody Marys. He could go to their room and have a Bloody Mary! Thank fucking Christ.

13

Dinner Parties

The big joke from the beginning was how, gee, maybe they should be home "working" on their marriage. "Working" on your marriage—it sounded as unappetizing as when those waiters asked "Are you still working on your salad, or just resting?" Whenever she heard that solemn phrase, she always envisioned couples in overalls with pickaxes rolling up their sleeves. Who would *want* to work on their marriage? Who knew how? Neither she nor Roger had any idea, but luckily it didn't matter. They had breezed into marriage as they had breezed into love—without a single use of the word "relationship."

This became another little joke. One time in Maine when they'd had the usual masses up for the weekend ("Scott and Zelda," her mother called them, as they appeared with enormous vats of beef bourguignon at the table Roger had made out of the old dock system), Roger had grumbled that he never got to spend any time alone with her. Lizzie was thrilled! Usually they never did get any time together; even when they were alone, Roger was always dashing up and down to the basement to fix something she didn't know was broken, cursing away.

Once, after a particularly virulent line of expletives, she'd
rushed out to the back porch and begged him to stop fixing whatever he was fixing, it was upsetting him so
much. "Upset? Upset? I've never been happier in my
life!" Roger had cried out. It was true! Changing the
hinges on a door made him happy, she had to accept it,
even though she had absolutely no understanding of the
concept. Her dream was to read books all day long, eating a broken-up bar of Turkish Taffy. There were certain
advantages, of course, to this quality of Roger's, she had
to admit as she lounged over *The Age of Innocence* one
Saturday afternoon, popping Italian green beans in her
mouth, while Roger loaded the car with enormous barrels for another run to the dump. The trick was—William
and she had nobly decided one evening playing rummy
on the deck in Maine to the *clang clang* of the twenty-
foot ladder Roger had suddenly, between gin and tonics,
appeared with to hang the outdoor thermometer—not to
let Roger's constant industry mar one's total indolence.
One (somehow it was always "one" when chatting with
William) had to allow Roger's drillings and poundings to
lull rather than disrupt, like a dishwasher churning comfortingly in the background. She finally realized there
was no changing Roger; even during the rare moments
she got him to sit still, driving in the car or something,
she would turn to him, *filled* with things to say, and
encounter that glazed look that meant he was tallying up
what he needed at the hardware store.

The only time Roger ever sat and relaxed was with
Guy, the hippie with the hair down his back who cut the
trees in Maine. All work would be suspended when Guy's
pickup crunched into the driveway, and for hours Roger
would sit with him on the deck, Roger's feet up on the
railing, wearing his baseball cap with the picture of the
chainsaw on the front. "What do you talk about all day

long?" Lizzie had asked. "You're always too busy to talk to me." She knew Roger thought he was being a hippie— Roger, who had missed the hippie era entirely, now thought all hippies were good. At least back when she had tried to be a hippie at age fifteen, if you met some- one in beads and long hair, he was pretty well guaranteed to be in favor of some kind of peaceful coexistence; nowadays if you were casting for *Woodstock*, your best bet would be to go directly to the correctional facilities of Massachusetts, where every rapist and serial killer wore a bandanna over cascading hair.

But that morning in Maine he'd mentioned that he wanted time alone with her! She was touched with romance. All day she imagined how, possibly (well, it *was* possible, wasn't it?) he would look into her eyes and gen- tly trace the outline of her nose with his finger, the way they did in the movies. And they would talk! She didn't know what about; she never knew *what* she wanted to say usually till halfway through the conversation. When- ever she dared say to Roger she wanted to talk, Roger would say "What about?" in this threatening kind of way and, *of course*, she'd be stumped. But what mattered was that they would be together alone, time on their hands, nothing to do but engage in the lazy give-and-take of thoughts, the sharing of hopes and dreams and fears, the barings of the soul. Well, maybe not Roger's soul, she couldn't quite go so far as to envision Roger baring his soul, but hers anyway—she was a great barer of the soul. Really, she said sighingly to herself, she couldn't wait. But what happened, when the time finally came and they'd left their guests and gone off to their room, was that Roger had grabbed her, made love to her, then immediately turned over to go to sleep. "I thought you wanted to spend some time alone with me!" she'd cried out, but Roger was already far away, plunged into sleep.

Roger maintained she'd have hated it if he'd been like those whiny guys at Harvard she'd known. True, all she'd done back in the days of her romance with Richard Townsend was "relate," moist-eyed looks ad infinitum, and where had it gotten her? Crying her eyes out on her electric blanket (could she get electrocuted? she'd sometimes wondered) while Richard Townsend went on relating with half the girls in Adams House. No, she didn't long for Richard Townsend anymore. And yet, sometimes in a weak moment, she wished she could occasionally have just a bit of the sincere-looks-in-the-eye malarkey from Roger to tide her over.

But of course, she *was* happy, totally happy. How this had happened to her, whose life had always been so convoluted, she did not know. It was just as she had always dreamed: Her marriage had taken over her life and made her happy. Married! Her whole life had been a series of dress rehearsals up to now. Ever since she could remember she'd been marrying something: her dog, her teddy bear, her brothers when they were asleep—on one wondrous fall day, she'd married a leaf. Now at last all her anxious drive was gone. She felt sleepy, in a good way, just thinking of it. How cozy to be married with the nights growing darker and the winter coming. She'd always loved looking at houses at night along a street, softly lit from within, everyone inside so happy and safe. At last, she was one of them.

She would come home at night now and whip up some cream sauce with frankfurters or something she'd found in one of Roger's bachelor cookbooks. She was making real cream sauces now—she'd had to, having received five crepe pans as wedding presents. Fondly she'd looked back on her early days, a year before, when she and Roger were first in love and it had taken her three days to make Quick Seafood Divan, which had consisted largely of combining Campbell's Cream of Chicken and Cream of Mushroom soups. Her learning to cook and the many gifts of china, of course, led to a situation rather like the armaments build up before World War I: the dinner party inevitably had followed.

Those dinner parties! She could hear her mother on the phone so excited to hear they were giving a dinner party. The dinner parties were comfy but boring, she had to admit, and yet she couldn't seem to resist them. She supposed it was the setting of the table that was so intoxicating, the salad plate on one side, the butter plate on the other—all administered to with the serious delight of a little girl giving a tea party. Banished would be the hundred-piece gas station china, offered by Texaco with their monthly billing, which Roger and his roommate had proudly purchased for $35 years before, indestructible plastic with a gridlike border around its circumference that astounded one with the fact that people had been paid first to design it, then to print it, china that went on and on in various plate, saucer, and bowl sizes. Out would come the wedding china (five complete sets!) and the four silver forks and so much cheese and crackers that you got sick before dinner, and at dinner the discussion about béchamel sauce, and when to get pregnant, the wine not a stimulant but a soporific.

She supposed she had become quite traditional. To the shock of all her friends she had even taken Roger's name. Frankly, "Reade" and "Stoner" were practically the same name anyway—if you put them together they sounded like a brokerage firm. Now she was "Elizabeth Stoner" as she started her new career. She wrote ads that got people to borrow money to buy things they hadn't known they wanted. Whether this could be considered, from the liberal point of view, as a step up or a step down from working against prisoners, she didn't know.

But Roger hadn't minded; once he'd swallowed denying those reformables their constitutional rights, the way was paved. No, Roger had bragged and bragged about her; he was as bad as her father. Roger was so *proud* of her after she got the job, and off she'd gone in her new little size-eight outfits charged at Saks—which was an investment, because if you looked like you knew what you were doing, people might start believing it—to spend her first week at work writing hundreds (and she meant *hundreds*—she could still see the pages of line after line) of headlines in the hopes of hitting the right one to "turn the people on," as the eager young account executive had put it so aptly, to the new revolutionary idea of writing yourself checks from lines of credit. "Write Yourself a Loan Whenever the Moment Grabs You!" was finally settled on after hours and hours of deliberation.

It was, in fact, her third career move in a year. How pleased the parents had been when she'd decided shortly after her wedding to become a schoolteacher—how soothing it had sounded and good for her marriage. She'd quit her job at the Department of Correction and signed up at Wellesley to get her masters and found herself writing papers that relied a bit heavily on the word "inherent." But she figured teaching school was the *perfect* job to have when you had kids—kids! She who had never baby-sat a day in her life, she who had never dreamed of having them, now was talking about kids! In her new married state the perks that the ignorant think are the boons of teachers—summers off, home by three, vacations at Christmas—danced like sugar plums in her head. She imagined students in class sunnily raising their hands with answers to her questions; she in a flattering brown skirt and yellow sweater, almost the age of her students, why the students might want to stay after class just to talk, the girls idolizing her for her ability to juggle career and marriage, the boys just a little in love with her, with her beauty and light heart, and then walking in the rustling fall leaves to the Subaru, a bit less battered now—had the boys in shop worked on it, perhaps?—and driving home in the late sunlight with just enough time to do the grocery shopping and cook something a little special for Roger, with a glass of Almaden and the candles lit in the brass candlesticks from, and profusely acknowledged as such, Aunt Cornelia.

Of course the reality was when she crawled away to her car humiliated and crying, to get home as fast as she could to hurl herself on the bed in a blackened bedroom with her very first migraine headache, dragging herself up the next morning at five o'clock to prepare for four classes of thirty-two children who put false names down on the attendance forms. She'd read through ten of them to titters of laughter—"Jacques Strap. Is Jacques Strap here, *please?*"—until she reached Mickey Mouse, and said sternly, "What the heck is going on?"

Then in the middle of her student teaching that June, she got a lump in her breast. The only good thing about those cancer scares was that you got all the credit of hovering near death and then everything would turn out to be benign. She might have had a mere two months to live the way she wielded this five-minute unnecessary incision as an excuse to get out of teaching forever, after trying it for just two months.

"I just feel the need to have children now," she explained solemnly, as if this naturally followed from not having cancer, to her student-teacher adviser from Wellesley, a motherly older woman who was urging her to stick with the teaching for another three months.

"And then, of course, we're thinking about maybe having children," she heard Roger explaining to a friend that August; they hadn't been married a year. Of course they'd never *talked* about having children; it was hard to have much of a discussion with someone who was laying sod under the tree and agreeing with everything you said. Not that she wasn't sure Roger was pleased at the idea; he loved her so much. Once she'd asked him out of the blue, "What in the world would you do without me?"

"I don't know," Roger had answered.

But when she'd arrived at the gynecologist, she suddenly chickened out. "Actually," she said to Roger upon her return, "what if we wait to have a baby?" and he'd said, "That's fine, it's completely up to you, I'm not the one giving up the career." The career! At the time her career was painting the walls of their apartment. He was being so nice about it. She couldn't help thinking she'd hurt him by not wanting a baby yet, he did love her so much. He never even got angry with her. Sometimes she almost wished he would. She wouldn't have minded a few sparks flying around to jazz things up, but how were you supposed to fight with a guy who thought everything you did was fine? Sometimes marriage felt like sitting on her father's lap.

Children? *Children?* She couldn't even make it down the street to get a gallon of milk without getting lost. When she'd sat him down in the half-painted living room—they'd moved to the apartment upstairs, which she'd been painting ever since quitting teaching and then not having cancer—and asked what if they tried to have a baby, what could he say? He'd never said anything but okay, great! He couldn't even admit that he didn't like a dress when she asked him *before* she bought it. When she'd had the cancer operation and he'd come to get her with her parents he hadn't known what to say or do. She'd been all weepy and upset, which would have been one thing if it had *been* cancer but since she had turned out to be fine, was he supposed to congratulate her or comfort her? He'd resorted to patting her comfortingly and smiling congratulatorily while she whimpered, and then when they'd gotten outside the front door of the hospital, she'd said, "I've forgotten my purse!" and he'd cried out, "I'll get it I'll get it!" thrilled to be able to do something active and leave all the psychological stuff to her parents.

"So, what do you think?" she'd said, having presented the baby idea. She had huge swathes of oil-base paint down her bare legs. Every night when he came home she was there rubbing turpentine all over her body. Children, children . . . Where had she come up with this ruinous idea?

"Great, great," he'd said, "it sounds great," and she'd run off to make the appointment to have what she called the UFO out.

As for the marriage, well, he would have had to admit it was as they said: The honeymoon was over. The house was always being vacuumed before people came over; guests were always coming, invited a week ahead. There were all sorts of lists around and cute notes affixed to his clothes that miraculously reappeared clean in his drawers. ("Put me out of my misery," said one of the T-shirts he'd cut a large scoop neck in so he could unbutton the top buttons of his shirts.) Furniture was always being moved around; his roommate's old room was now the "den." Lizzie began setting her hair, sitting under a huge bonnetted hair dryer. They had two drinks a night instead of a hundred.

All the crazy times were over, and, except for Lizzie's floundering in her career, which didn't affect him one way or the other, they were settling in. Sex on Saturday nights after the dishes were done. Hanging out at the houses of other married people who had suddenly become their friends since they'd gotten married. A bunch of lawyers in a stifling hot room. He had absolutely nothing to say to these people. They never even left the dining-room table all evening, but would sit in straightback chairs crammed around in a circle oohing and aahing over some seven-goddamn-layered crepe, with a long discussion of what went in each layer, and then out would come the *cranberry* tart, nobody budging and then, just as he was motioning to Lizzie to leave, proudly from the kitchen would come the husband with the water-processed decaffeinated coffee. They couldn't even have caffeine in their coffee anymore.

But everyone else sat there as happy as could be. Even Lizzie, who had never gotten along with women, was suddenly the belle of the ball amongst the wives, discussing cookbooks. Lizzie in wide-legged hostess pants and low heels. What had happened to the girl in the denim short-shorts and knotted shirt ("Daisy-mae," he'd called her that first summer)? Now she was just one of the wives. Well, the last thing he wanted to be was one of the husbands. The men were worse than the women; half the time he had to pretend to be interested in how they'd made the lemon-ginger sauce (which had tasted *precisely* like furniture polish).

Did anyone ever suggest they rise from that table and go find a Ping-Pong table, or, at the very least, some more comfortable seats to be bored in? No, there they would all sit, staring at one another, Roger's eyes watering with trying to come up with something to say, until finally he would excuse himself and flee to the bathroom. The bathroom—it was his favorite place on a Saturday night. He would stand there deeply sighing for as long as he thought he could get away with, flushing the toilet a couple of times for veracity, before dragging himself back to the table—they were still at the table, that was a guarantee, riveted by the surprise twist the discussion had taken away from coffee filters to bouillon cubes.

What had happened to all the kicking up your heels and dancing? If they weren't at dinner parties, they were staying at home nights to a home-cooked meal. Half the time they ate in the dining room, now painted, in the third attempt to reach "china red," a Pepto-Bismol pink. When he'd first met Lizzie, she couldn't boil water without burning the pot. Now she was always at the stove in some godforsaken hand-me-down apron from his mother. Who wanted a home-cooked meal every night? Some nights he longed for a Stouffer's for four on a bed of Minute Rice. He didn't want to be waited on; his mother had always waited on his father hand and foot, with one-sided chitchat, as his father sat silently drinking his coffee. No, he didn't want Lizzie to cook, but if she cooked, he thought it only fair that he at least do the dishes, with the result that he felt all too often like William Bendix, a dish towel hanging over his arm.

He was vastly relieved when she got the job in advertising and fell in with a drinking crowd. It meant he didn't have to come home right after work every night. Jesus, even work had become a little boring that year; the documentary money had dried up along with Watergate, and producing a news show every day hadn't been enough to keep him interested. In August he began to work full-time for "The Cafe," a live talk show during which the studio was turned into a bar open to the public. "The Cafe" was everything he liked—drinking and television rolled into one. Well, almost everything; he wasn't sure how moving or socially redeeming those segments on reducing your thighs exactly were. Still, he thought it was great that PRV was doing something unpretentious. Originally he had planned to stay with the news and just do segments for "The Cafe," then he'd substitute-hosted, then hosted full-time, and finally been asked to produce the show as well.

His favorite night of the week was Tuesday, when they taped all five shows, boom, boom, one after another—you never had a second to think about what you were doing. At the end of taping (he wouldn't touch a drop beforehand) he'd say to the bartender, "Pour me a beer, will you, and start tossing them down."

One Tuesday night in September, after the show was over, he picked up the phone and dialed a number off the top of his head. He didn't think about it, he wouldn't have dreamed of thinking about it, he just picked up the phone and called Joyce. There was only one reason to call Joyce.

And yet, it wasn't as if Roger had thought to himself, Well, this is it, I guess I'm about to cheat on my marriage, he'd just dialed the number. Joyce was the woman who had always filled in the gaps between girlfriends, one of the blonds he'd met at Brandy's who never made any pretense about there needing to be a relationship. He hadn't spoken to Joyce since she'd called him two years before and he'd told her he was in love. He'd still been in the early-Lizzie period, when he tended to refer to their plans in the first person singular. "I'm going up to Maine this weekend," he'd mentioned conversationally on the phone. "And where will *I* be going this weekend?" Lizzie had asked, breezing by.

That night he simply broke the two-year silence with a "hi, let's get together, what do you want to do?" Probably he could have simply said "Let's go to bed" to Joyce, but of course he hadn't admitted to himself that those were his intentions.

They wound up going to some movie, then out for drinks, and then it was, gee, well, let's go back to your place. She had a condominium in Brookline, near the travel agency, or was it a real estate agency, where she worked, he couldn't remember. Sadly, he was not racked with any great pangs of guilt afterward, or any little pangs for that matter. The most that could be said was that when he drove into his driveway and saw the light upstairs, he didn't feel particularly good.

14

Save Me

They'd been married a year. To celebrate, they dressed up and drove further into the suburban wilds to eat at a restaurant with a French name that would have been ridiculous had it been in English. Roger, blow-dried and looking like a quiz-show host in the "continental" suit he'd bought for "The Cafe," had, after a gander at the prices, promptly eaten everything in sight and was now smiling blandly—nothing to say! Well, she supposed anniversaries were a bit like New Year's, just a little too much pressure to be romantic, but still, *nothing* to talk about? They *used* to have plenty to say, not about anything particularly earth-shattering, of course, but never had there been a second of silence between them when they were together—where had the back-and-forth gone? At least he was smiling. In the last few weeks he'd gotten so *serious*; still at his projects, but now when he charged around the house carrying a crowbar to rip down an attic wall, he looked ominous, as if he were angry at something, though never with her—no, never with her, everything was always just fine, whatever she wanted.

No, she couldn't complain about his treatment of her.

Still, what was he suddenly so serious about? Certainly not work—he'd gone from producing stories about busing in South Boston to introducing cooking segments, for goodness' sake. So why the long face? She'd married a professed bon vivant, and now he went around looking grim all the time. Well, there was no point in discussing it; it was their anniversary after all. So they'd driven home and were asleep by ten.

And then everything changed. She didn't know why, but suddenly, instead of going home every night after work to cook dinner, she found herself sailing out with the crowd to Copley's for a drink, each time feeling a little more guilty. Not that Roger minded of course. No, Roger actually approved of her going out, she guessed, because he approved of all drinking. Now when she thought back on it, she suspected the secret to their stunning courtship was that they'd been drunk the entire time. She remembered that first morning in Bermuda, in a brief sober moment, looking across the hotel breakfast table at Roger—nearly unrecognizable to her at that distance (for three straight days, she'd known him only in extreme close-up), his hair slicked back from the shower—and thinking to herself, Who is this guy? But now here she was drinking again, and without Roger. Worse, sometimes as she listened to the conversations of her new colleagues—so bright and irreverent, especially in the light of each new gin and tonic—she found herself wondering if maybe she had made a mistake marrying so young. Of course she loved Roger, but sometimes she worried that maybe she'd married just a tad beneath herself, in that Roger wasn't exactly an intellectual.

Not like Miller Cross, her creative group head. Miller Cross was quite the intellectual, meaning he paid attention to her, in that intelligent way men had when they wanted to sleep with you. She would sit at the shining brass bar at Copley's, jabbering away as Miller Cross regarded her with intent eyes, suddenly interrupting her, as if he could not help himself, saying, "You're very pretty, you know." She knew he said it to everyone, she got him to admit he said it to everyone, but somehow it didn't matter, it wasn't necessary to really believe it, it was enough that someone had bothered to say it at all.

Soon she was going out almost every night, hating herself for it, but unable to resist it. Weeks and then months of swaying out to lobby phones to call Roger, slurrily informing him that she'd be home in one hour, two hours, three hours—Roger still didn't seem to mind. Not even the night when she'd arrived home at 1:00 A.M., flushed, to face Roger with all the buttons of her overcoat torn off—flushed from being kissed by Miller Cross in the *bushes* in front of the Copley Plaza.

How it had happened, she was no longer certain— she'd been horribly drunk, but she seemed to remember a preliminary scene of the two of them exchanging a little kiss at the table in the bar to a gentle applause. "We're made for each other," Cross had said, "both married!" Oh, God. Of course she'd fancied herself in love by the time they'd reached the bushes. As he'd pulled her toward him she'd beseeched him to bring her candies in a heart-shaped box the following day, Valentine's Day, and he had promised, between the branches, with great gallantry and quotings of Shakespeare. She'd gone to bed that night next to Roger, full of a flowering love for Miller Cross. Then the next day, Cross had ignored her, totally ignored her, and she'd sheepishly gone out and bought Roger, who didn't wear them, a pair of pajamas.

But it wasn't just Miller Cross. (How much easier it would have been to justify one fatal love outside her marriage!) Apparently, others would do. For instance, Tom Koch, who cropped up early that April out of nowhere—well, not nowhere exactly, because he had always been around. For the last two years they'd developed a couples' relationship: she'd invited him and his wife to their wedding, to the cabin in Maine, and so forth. Why Roger put up with it, she couldn't say; certainly he made no special effort to conceal his true feelings for Tom. "You're just about enough of an asshole to last a lifetime" he'd actually said to Tom, casually over New Year's Eve dinner. But now suddenly there was no pretense of couples, Tom having called her for a drink, as if he knew the rules had changed—picking her up at work, waiting for her at the front desk for all to see, in a French tie, looking darkly, adulterously handsome. But almost immediately the drama was dissipated by the usual grapplings over which bar to choose, and when finally they arrived at some dreadful anonymous dive, he proved as surly as usual, and, having forgotten his wallet again, impossible to love.

Well, *almost* impossible. When he stopped the car to drop her home, she leaned toward him across the front seat, until she was in his embrace, sinking into him, thinking over and over again, Save me, save me, save me. From what she did not know.

That Friday night they loaded the dogs in the car and drove to Maine having, for some reason, a sprightly discussion about the possibility of Roger getting a job in New York, how he could commute weekends for the first six months. Somehow this segued into Roger saying as they opened the door to the cabin, "Let's face it, our sex life is not what you'd exactly call great."

"I'll divorce you! I'll divorce you!" she'd screamed for a while, much to her surprise, since all during the previous conversation she'd been thinking about how free she would be with Roger in New York. But then, oddly, everything had quieted down, and for the rest of the weekend not a single allusion was made to the fight that had almost happened.

On the way home, she'd said, "Let's stay home next weekend and smoke some dope and talk." She hadn't liked smoking pot since her sophomore year in high school, but something instinctively told her it was time to be a little more of a hippie instead of an advertising writer who wore suits and dried her hair in curlers. But then Eric, her friend from college, called to say he was coming for the weekend, and by the time he left it was Sunday, and she had this dinner party she had had to plan two months ahead to get her old high school teacher and college roommate together, who she'd just known would get along so well. She had foreseen such a hilarious evening, but in the end everyone left by nine, and then there was Roger methodically doing the dishes. "Oh, leave them!" she said, "and come to bed." "No," said Roger grimly, "I'd like to finish." And though she waited for him upstairs in the attic bedroom, Roger, who was generally a soaker, scrubbed and scoured until at last she fell asleep.

So Monday was the big night. "Got to go home and work on the relationship" she told her friends at work, but then a group of them decided to go out for a quick drink and then another, while she kept calling home to reach Roger. He wasn't there! Well, at least she didn't feel quite so bad that *she* was out drinking. Finally around ten she got him on the phone.

"Where have you been?" she asked, but not accusingly.

"Out drinking."

"With whom?"

"No one. Just thinking"

Thinking! Roger? She didn't like the sound of it.

He came and picked her up. She felt like a bad girl who was being brought home by her father. My, he was serious tonight. She had been serious, too, for the past week. Hadn't she sent him that nice note (she thought it was rather poetic): "My heart is breaking" and she kept meaning to ask if he had received it. She was ready to go back to the marriage; not that she'd ever, even in the throes of love in the bushes, ever considered leaving Roger, *ever*—she would never hurt him like that! This had all been some horrible six-month aberration, and she would make it all right again.

They drove home in silence. She guessed there weren't going to be any jokes about working on the relationship tonight. She heaved a deep sigh; it wasn't going to be any fun, but she supposed she deserved it. She would gladly make amends. She had discovered she loved Roger after all, realized it suddenly when she'd flown into a rage in Maine. How lovely to discover she loved the man she was married to. Admittedly convincing him of her renewed love might be a bit more difficult than she anticipated. She suspected, whether he knew it or not, that he'd closed himself off from her because she'd hurt him too much with her flirting. And yet, why was she still so reluctant to talk about it? Well, of course, her recent activities weren't her favorite scenes to relive; certainly, even muscling all her powers of self-deception, she could not convince herself that she'd acted altogether in a noble way.

Sitting in the silence of the Peugeot, she wondered again how much it was really necessary to confess to Roger. Why upset him with the facts? She had once read in *Cosmopolitan* that there was no need to confess an affair to your spouse because it would just haunt them, and then, of course, she hadn't even had an affair!

When they got home Roger led her to the den as if they were to look upon an open casket. They sat down and Roger spoke the line that she instantly knew had been going round and round his head all night.

"It's just not working out," Roger said as if in conclusion.

"What do you mean?" she said, suddenly terrified.

"It's just not working out," he repeated firmly, avoiding her eyes.

That was *it*? That was all he was going to say? Now at last, she knew what she needed saving from: Roger was leaving her, he was leaving her! "Please don't leave me. Please don't leave me!" she cried out, falling clumsily to her knees as if to illustrate the rug being pulled out from under her. My God. What had she done? He couldn't just leave her like that, could he? Could he? Not if she begged him on her knees!

"Please don't leave me! Please!" she kept sobbing over and over. She couldn't think of anything else to say. She couldn't seem to move him, not to comfort her, not even to look at her. He just sat there, his face hardening against every plea.

"I love you," she said, finally, brilliantly. He couldn't leave her if she loved him, could he? He must have thought she didn't really love him, all that time, that was it! "I love you!" she tried again.

He didn't want to talk about it. He just had this urgent need to bolt. He would feel sorry for her if he could—he didn't dislike her, he wished to God almighty he did!—but all he could feel was: when could he get the goddamn hell out of there? How long were you supposed to sit there letting them sob? This was worse than he'd expected. Not that he'd known any of this was going to happen until it happened—he hadn't said to himself, I'll take Lizzie home and tell her I'm leaving her. He had just thought over and over all night at the bar, and then the whole time while driving Lizzie home: It's just not working out. But it was when he said the phrase out loud to Lizzie that he knew, knew in a flash: he was leaving her, he was leaving her that night, as soon as he could get out.

"Let me go upstairs for a minute," she cried. "Promise you won't go yet?"

"Okay," he agreed. What else could he say? He supposed it was all part of his punishment.

She just needed a little time to figure out how to get him to stay. You could always get a guy to stay, with a guy there were all sorts of ways. Once he left it would be all over; she had to get him to reconsider! She ran up the stairs, still crying, but not figuring anything out. "Oh God, oh God, oh God" was the best she could come up with. What was she going to do? This couldn't be happening to her, it was everything she had always dreaded, all her life—being abandoned. But they'd told her it was an *irrational* dread, the shrinks, irrational that she felt abandoned when the dentist left town, irrational that she felt abandoned when someone she didn't particularly like canceled lunch. And she'd believed them, in spite of all her fears, she'd believed them—she hadn't ever expected to be *really* abandoned, and certainly not by her husband.

Tears still streaming, she changed out of her advertising clothes, suddenly blaming them. She got into her nightgown, some stupid Lanz flannel nightgown with vertical lines of little pink flowers and a square line of ruffles outlining the bust, a Christmas present from her mother-in-law. Inspirationally, she thought to wake up her parents with the news. "Hi Mom, Roger's leaving, Roger's leaving!!" she blurted out over the phone. They tried to calm her down; it will be better in the morning, they said. "But he's leaving *now*," she wept, "right now, he can't wait!" She was trying to hold back the tears when she went back down the stairs into the den. As Roger stood up, she saw that he was holding his toilet case!

"Oh no!" she pleaded. "Please, don't go, not tonight," but it was clear he was leaving, in spite of her groveling. She followed him to the door.

"I thought you adored me!" she said. But as she looked up at his face, at last it occurred to her that, no, no, on the contrary, he did not.

15

The Wrong Person

He had just married the wrong person, that was all. He'd
made an honest mistake and he was just trying to correct
it. That was all. He should have married a hippie. He
should have *been* a hippie! A hippie was relaxed, not
driven on the weekend—well, he supposed, not really
driven anytime. He had always marveled at people who
could just hang out. Like Guy, the tree-chopper in Maine.
Guy could sit staring at the trees, smoking a joint, doing
nothing for hours on end. Not, of course, that on a general basis Roger wasn't *miserable* if he wasn't accom-
plishing something at every turn. Every day was a contest
with him, to see how much he could get done, and it was
never enough. No, he knew in his heart that he never
could have been much of a hippie. And yet, a part of him
wished he had a little of the hippie in him, wished he had
had the courage to do nothing, get nothing done in a day,
just hang out, grow his hair long, say "fuck you" to the
world. He had never even grown his hair! The one time
at age twenty-five he'd gone out on a limb and grown a
mustache, a picture had been taken of him with his
mother, and she forever looked at it and said with great

hilarity, "Now there's the picture of that nice middle-aged couple."

All he knew was that the marriage wasn't working. He'd gotten married too quickly, hadn't really known who Lizzie was. He'd married a girl in tights and ballet shoes and wild hair and ended up with a girl who could have stepped out of Greenwich, Connecticut. He remembered watching her model those clothes from Saks, with the gathered skirts and full bodices that obscured all outline of the body, and thinking, Who does she think she's buying those for? Not that he was jealous of her new friends—he wished in a way that he was—it was just that this person bustling off to a career in advertising wasn't what he'd ever had in mind.

His marriage, he had come to see, had been the same as selling life insurance, that terrifying twelve months when he'd said to himself that he couldn't believe that this was what he would be doing for the rest of his life. Knocking on some guy's door and virtually pushing yourself into his living room. But he had refused to accept it as his fate and quit his job. You could quit a job, of course, but you weren't supposed to quit a marriage. Still, he'd seen his father walk out on a marriage. So it *could* be done. It might not be good, or right, but it sure as hell was possible.

What's more, he could do it and go on with his life, just as he had always done, without a glance backward. It just *felt* better to not dwell on things, it was the way he'd been brought up, it was a good strategy in a household where your father hated your mother. And of course, much as he preferred not to think about that one, he knew that his mother's avoidance of the fact of his father's feelings had set the tone for much of his childhood. Not that after the divorce his mother always kept things in, at least not about his father—she was always ready with a dig or two. His father was the villain, according to his mother, and how could Roger not admit to seeing her point of view, although the problem was, when he saw his father, he not only didn't hate him, he actually liked him, and for that matter, he even liked Mrs. Ash. He felt guilty about it, guilty every time he had to leave his mother to go over and have a scotch at Mrs. Ash's, and he couldn't help thinking about it now.

Now he was a villain, just like his father. His mother had shown him a letter his mild-mannered, generous father had written her shortly after he'd walked out. Talk about cold—my God, the letter was as cold as ice, to his mother, totally surprised at the breakup, at the fact of Mrs. Ash, devastated after twenty-six years of marriage. Well, Roger was getting out after a year and a half, surely that was better, a little better?

He hadn't had any strong feelings leaving Lizzie, even as she'd been crying on her knees—not love, not hate, not even, really, pity. Although he had hated selling life insurance, he had never, not once, hated Lizzie; he hadn't even disliked her. It would have been so much easier if they'd had fights or something! He remembered what his father had said when Roger had stood before his desk that Christmas vacation, his sophomore year at Exeter. He had specifically asked Roger to stop in at the office that afternoon, but Roger hadn't thought anything of it, just swung in from his way back from the Whitmarshes.

"Your mother and I are getting divorced," his father had said.

"But why?" Roger had asked, getting a sinking feeling down to his toes. Of course he had known for years, intuitively, and then for certain, about Mrs. Ash, he had known and prayed his mother would never know. And yet he was surprised.

"Your mother and I just can't seem to agree," his

father had explained, adding, as Roger rose to walk out, "And Rog, let's just keep this between the two of us." His father hadn't yet spoken with his mother; he'd told Roger first. And then that very night had come the news that his brother was getting engaged, and his father had postponed telling his mother for two years. And for two years, Roger had waited, hoping his father would change his mind.

"Your mother and I just can't seem to agree." Of course that just might have been an excuse. He'd never seen his parents exchange more than a few sentences, what could they have disagreed on, please pass the jelly? He remembered being eleven when David had gotten on the plane to Choate, and it had just been him and his mother and father at dinner that night. What the hell had his parents done when he'd gone away to school? he wondered.

Anyway, he had felt tight looking at Lizzie suffering, she'd once told him about this fear of abandonment she had. Her mother had been taken away to the mental hospital for two years right after she'd had Lizzie, and she'd been shipped around as an infant to various aunts. Well, he was sorry that had happened, and he was sorry he was doing it to her again, and yet he'd felt that sorrow only in a detached way, as if she were in some story he was reading in the paper. Most of his energy had gone into trying to leave, get far away from the possibility of having to talk about any of it, but toward her suffering, he'd felt horribly matter-of-fact.

He took off everything but his underwear and crawled into the bed in the crummy little motel room— the Ma and Pa Motel that his mother always stayed at (always so thrifty—her original hope was to be allowed to sleep in some cobwebbed corner of his attic)—thinking: I can't believe I've done it. He'd left Lizzie.

In the middle of the night he woke up and started punching himself in the face, trying to feel something or to punish himself for having done something wrong. He didn't know which.

16

Alternate Nights

Three days later they were meeting at the lawyer's to sign the purchase and sale on a town house in Back Bay Boston. They'd found a four-story town house to buy about a month earlier, or rather Lizzie had. She'd seen the ad for the house in the paper (he hadn't known they were looking), gone to see it, brought Roger in the next day, and the deed was done. Had he known at the time that he was going to walk out? The one thing he had known was that he didn't want to leave Watertown and the house he'd bought when he was twenty-seven and put so much of himself into. The only rebellion he'd ever had was living in a blue-collar town (albeit, he had to admit, in a large Victorian high on the hill, a castle lording it over the neighborhood of three-decker houses). Watertown represented the kind of people he wanted to know; Back Bay represented going back to Greenwich, Connecticut, moving back toward his upbringing instead of away from it. And yet, he'd gone along, never even hinting to Lizzie that he didn't want to move. Well, he'd never been able to say no to her, and then, he was a practical man, and he'd reasoned the two-family town house was a good investment. "Why an eight percent variable mortgage instead of an eight and three-quarter percent fixed?" William, who was now their lawyer, having left PRV the year before, had asked Roger over the phone. "Because I don't expect to own the house long," Roger had said. Even before he'd known he was leaving Lizzie, he'd known he'd be leaving that house in Back Bay.

"You have to promise you'll come with me to see a marriage counselor," Lizzie had said calmly on the phone the morning after he'd walked out.

"Okay," he'd agreed to mollify her; true to her background, she needed the experts to corroborate. Then they'd made plans to get together for supper that night. For some unknown reason, he'd wanted to see her.

As he had watched her cry in the car outside Charlie's Eating and Drinking Saloon, he'd felt—what, pity? It wasn't much, but it was something. He'd felt sorry for her, sorry he was hurting her. He told her (to his surprise) that he loved her; unlike he had to other women, he had never said I love you to Lizzie and not meant it. But it didn't mean he was coming back. She didn't understand this—how could he expect her to understand it? He didn't understand it himself.

"I just don't love you that way," he'd said.

"What way?" she'd asked, as they'd headed up Storrow Drive. "The way a husband should love a wife," he'd said. It was then she'd flung her wedding ring out the window.

"Oh, Lizzie," he'd said, "why did you do that?" He drove her home—home?—patted Hope and Leslie, gave her a kiss. She was still crying. He'd told her not to worry, he'd go with her to the marriage counselor. Not to worry? He had absolutely no intention of going to that marriage counselor more than once, twice maximum—he was only going as a token gesture. He knew without asking that the so-called "marriage counselor" was really some kind of shrink Lizzie was slipping in on him. Well, no shrink was going to convince him he was crazy just because he had left his wife. No, the marriage just hadn't worked out, and what could be saner than recognizing that fact early on?

On the second night when they'd gotten together, he knew he didn't really love her, he had only thought so out of pity, there was no hope. That night he'd felt nothing when she cried; he'd known he was doing the right thing.

So now, as they were breaking up they were buying a big beautiful town house in Back Bay. "So Lizzie can walk to work," he had told his family, four weeks back.

Four weeks back, she had stood at the bedroom window and looked down at the gas-lit street and thought, This is my home! This was Back Bay, where her family had lived for generations! Where her mother and grandmother had been born. Where she had ridden the swanboats as a little girl. Where as a young woman at Harvard she had come those terrible Friday afternoons, dressed to the nines (but always in the wrong thing), to have lunch with old Mrs. Eliot and young Mrs. Harland (a mere seventy) at Great-Aunt Elizabeth's before symphony, which her great-aunt abhorred but religiously attended every Friday of her life, sitting with gloved fingers in her ears during the "modern music." Symphony! Which Lizzie had hated also, feeling so strange among the girls there her age, dressed like her mother's generation in short loden jackets, with thick golden hair and fat golden earrings. But she had always gone when her great-aunt had an extra ticket—in her family it would have been a sin to admit you didn't like symphony—and endured the

society and hard wooden seats, wishing she belonged
there on the one hand and glad she didn't on the other.

And yet, for all her misgivings, Back Bay was her her-
itage, and at last she was there in her own right. Looking
down at the brick sidewalks that day, she'd felt so
rooted, so happy.

Now, four weeks later, she was in Back Bay sitting
anxiously in a lawyer's office. Roger was patting her
hand consolingly, as William, who, along with the rest of
the world (except her fortunate parents), knew nothing
of their three-day-old split, had walked into the confer-
ence room with the papers. "Love birds," he'd said,
shaking his head.

There was something so awful about signing all those
papers and yet, she could never be around lawyers without getting giggly. They were always so *official*, especially
in this case, with the lawyer on the opposing side, a
woman all frumped up in a busy suit, bustling about and
speaking sharply to some young female lackey about the
coffee, and eyeing everyone suspiciously, as if they were
all conspiring to cheat her. To top it off the woman was a
personal friend of William's, working at a firm one floor
down, and still she refused to honor the check of his
firm. "Aren't you glad I'm not a lawyer?" Lizzie wrote
on a little scrap of paper and slipped it to Roger.

Finally came the moment when they had to sign in all
the checked places. That was the worst—she always got
nervous when she had to sign her name in front of Roger,
who inevitably had an impatient, irritated look on his
face because her signature was so bad, a squiggle and
three horizontal lines. Half the time she'd get so flustered
she'd even screw *that* up, putting in an extra horizontal
line or something, and when she'd start to mention it,
Roger would grab the paper from her, saying it didn't
matter, nobody could read a goddamn word she wrote

anyway, her handwriting was a crime against humanity.

But of course, Roger *had* to be nice to her that day about her signature, though she could see him swallowing his chagrin. "I feel like we're getting divorced!" was the next clever crack out of her mouth. But they weren't—he was going to work on the marriage, he promised he'd come with her to the marriage counselor's. He had to try because he loved her; at least *today* he loved her. It was the night *before* he didn't love her. She had to get the days straight. This was an alternate night, he loved her on alternate nights—it was *last* night that the cold streak she had sometimes discerned in him was in full flame, if a cold streak could be in full flame. And so, after the lawyer's, off they went like a pair of newlyweds to the merry-go-round bar at the Hyatt Regency to drink, no one merrier, laughing as they watched her purse, which she'd thrown down to the floor in her usual way, go round and round three revolutions before they'd gotten hold of it.

They were smashed by 7:30; he drove her back to Watertown and said he'd call her later that night, as if he couldn't get enough of her.

He called around ten—or she thought it was ten. She had passed out up in the bedroom next to the fancy clock radio Roger's father had so proudly given them the Christmas before. She loved Roger's father, but she hated that clock radio. One night at 3:00 it had just popped itself to "on," of its own accord, jarring them awake to John Denver singing "Rocky Mountain Highhhhh" at top volume. They hadn't even been able to shut the radio off by unplugging it, the damn thing had some battery-operated power thing so you could hear John Denver during a tornado or whatever—a miraculous mechanism that, she noticed, had conveniently stopped working the night Roger had walked out, when for some reason the radio had come unplugged. She'd come home the next day to all sorts of flashing red lights, and then of course she hadn't a clue how to change it to the right time. As a result, she had had to keep a little pad of paper next to the bed in order to compute the time.

Roger was calling from the Cattle Call, the tavern where the PRV crowd hung out; she could hear the noise in the background. He was very sweet and seemed to be in a very excited, accommodating mood, like a little boy who was being so good because he was getting his way. Call him anytime, he said, he'd be at the Ma and Pa Motel.

She hung up, feeling dozy and happy, thinking idly that his mood reminded her of something, and drifted off to sleep.

She woke up with a start a few hours later to the smell of her Shake 'n Bake burning one floor below and the realization, as sharp as a poker in her side, of what Roger's mood reminded her of: the mood she'd been in when she'd called *him* up from Copley's right before she'd gone off into the bushes with Miller Cross. Oh God. It was somewhere past midnight, but she didn't care. She picked up the phone and called Roger's motel. "Not in," the guy at the desk reported. She felt sick; everything inside was caving in. She went to the phonebook and looked up her name: Jean Stock. There it was.

In Brighton of course, she would live in Brighton, everyone at PRV righteously lived in that dingy Brighton, until the old trust funds kicked in and they quietly made the move to the expensive woods of Lincoln. She probably had a cat. She would.

Not, of course, that she really knew a single fact about her. She had only heard her name twice. Three or four months earlier, when Roger had casually mentioned there were two new string reporters at the station, two young girls, kind of cute, he'd said, but in a patronizing way, and then later that winter had been the phone call Lizzie had answered, asking for Roger, who at the time was in the attic cutting a hole in the roof.

"This is Jean Stock," the fresh, out-of-breath voice had informed her. "Could you just tell Roger I got tickets to the game after all, and I'll catch him at the half?"

"I sure will," she'd said.

"You're jealous, aren't you?" Roger had said, amused when she'd relayed the message. The thing was, she really hadn't been, but those were the days she'd thought he'd adored her. Now all she could think of was Jean Stock, no-nonsense in her cords and jeans, no frills and long, straight, too-thin mousy hair—she had never seen her, but she knew this somehow—not even pretty, but certainly hip. She liked the Celts, did she? She liked Roger, *that's* who she'd liked. He was with Jean Stock right now and he was taking off her clothes, her corduroys and plaid shirt. She knew it. She stared at Jean Stock's number, but instead she called the motel every half hour, enhancing her humiliation by her explanation to the guy at the desk (who was singularly unimpressed) with "I'm his wife!" and then, finally at 4:00 A.M., begging him, "Please go down and knock on his door!" She waited breathlessly for her reward of "Nope, not in."

"I'm really pissed at that guy, I was there all night, he must have been ringing the wrong room," Roger said over the phone to her at work that morning. Really, really, she said; she was so relieved. The one thing she knew was that Roger never lied.

Besides, she was confident everything was going to be all right, because that night they were going to the marriage counselor. The marriage counselor would have to be on her side, wouldn't he? That was his business, after all, trying to keep marriages together. She was only sorry she hadn't gotten Dr. Trumbull, who'd been Spencer's shrink long ago at Brookhill and who had grown up with Mrs. Andrews in Dover. But he had been going on one of those exotic trips her parents and their friends were always embarking on to places like Greenland or Kenya (the year before, her father the nature-hater had been forced to look at birds all day and sleep in a tent next to a herd of rhinoceros—"they usually don't make trouble," the guide had assured him), and had referred her to Dr. Carsy.

It was May by now, that damn springtime when she always wanted to be in a white dress going to her senior prom, but had generally been overweight and depressed. Well, she wasn't overweight now—for the first time in her life she'd gotten her wish to get skinny when unhappy instead of looking like a stuffed chipmunk. She hadn't been able to eat a thing since Roger left; the tragedy was, she was so jittery she couldn't enjoy being thin. Carsy, she was happy to note, was affiliated with Brookhill, but saw most of his private patients out of his suburban house in Lexington, which was just as well, considering Roger's view of shrinks. No, Roger probably wouldn't have been wild about driving into Brookhill and seeing the nutcases walking around the hills with glazed expressions. *She* found it homey, of course, but the important thing was Roger. She knew Roger would eventually come to like seeing a shrink, in spite of his prejudices; how could he not? Shrinks always made you feel so great about having the worst, most murderous thoughts—well, now that she was actually thinking about it, she didn't know how much she wanted Roger feeling good about what he'd done. But whatever his response, she was sure that he would open up, cry, and talk about his mixed feelings, and by the session's end they would return home together clutching each other in gentle grief.

But everything was all wrong. Dr. Carsy was a little too brilliantly silver-haired and slightly unctuous, and he certainly wouldn't have grown up with Mrs. Andrews in Dover. As they sat in his paneled basement, Roger, having chosen a chair quite a distance from her, had gone suddenly from being very nice in the car to cold and hostile. And Carsy, instead of being all sympathy and understanding, started right off the bat with, "Have either of you been unfaithful?" There was a second's pause, while she considered the technicalities of her case.

"No," they both said in unison. Dr. Carsy looked mildly disappointed, but Lizzie could tell he had something on his mind that was bucking him up, and sure enough, he soon got round to it.

"Well," he said, "often in these cases it's good to be seen separately, and,"—here he took a prideful breath—"my wife has just gotten her social worker degree!" The next thing they knew in stepped Mrs. Carsy from the wings, a round, white-haired woman who should have been home baking cookies for Santa's elves but instead, with bright, eager eyes, plopped herself down between Roger and Lizzie, all ready and raring to talk about S-E-X. "Perhaps," said Dr. Carsy with a glint, "our next session we could divide up; say, Roger come to me and you, Elizabeth, to my wife?"

No sirree Bob, she was thinking to herself, but instead she'd said she'd consider it, in order to get back to the business of things.

Where, she wondered, were all the "Let's work on the relationship" discussions? Instead, Roger kept going on and on about things against her right there in the office, in front of two strangers! He, who had never criticized her in his life. It was like having your brother not stand up for you on the playground.

"I can't say no to her," he said. She could not help

thinking maybe this wasn't necessarily *that* bad a fault. "I can't even fucking tell her I don't like the dress she's got on."

Then: "She can't *do* anything. She can't drive to the dry cleaners without getting lost."

"I thought you thought that was kind of cute," she'd volunteered, to receive only a withering glance.

And then the constant refrain: "I've never been close to anybody in my life!" How about now, she kept saying, isn't this a good time to start? At least, she thought wildly to herself, he's never been close to anyone else. But it was small consolation. When they left the shrink he was still cold, angry, a million miles away.

"So when are you coming over to talk?" she asked in the car. She knew it was a bad time to bring it up, but she couldn't help herself.

"Friday, I guess," he said. She wished he could have summoned up a little enthusiasm if only to be polite, but she supposed everything would be all right once they got together and talked.

She knew these things took time. On Friday, she and her husband would sift through things, then maybe go out to dinner. Perhaps he would spend the weekend. They could go slow, not even sleep together until they were ready. Sunday was Easter. They could drive out to her parents'; they'd been signed up by her mother since January. When she'd been little and everyone else was getting Easter baskets with stuffed bunnies and toys, there'd been no fuss about Easter in the house; she couldn't even remember Easter as a child. But now that all of them were grown-up it was, "What time are you coming out on Easter?" from her mother, directly after opening the Christmas presents. She wouldn't expect much if Roger would stay the weekend; the point was they would be *trying*, trying is always what mattered, and they would be coming back to each other bit by bit.

Friday night she got home at 5:00, in time to wash her hair and dry it before Roger's arrival. But she'd forgotten Roger would be leaving work early to keep a four o'clock appointment with Dr. Carsy, and so he'd appeared at 5:30 to view her sitting in curlers under the bonnetted hair dryer. He had just said something she couldn't hear as she lifted the hood with a startled cry.

"I had an affair," Roger repeated.

17

Roger Confesses

Surprise, surprise—every minute was a new surprise; it was getting to be like Christmas. Now she learned, as she sat in the living room ripping out the last roller, that sex between Roger and her had never been good. He had never thought of her as sexy. Was she a moron? What about their early lusty days? Sex was her whole thing; she was the one guys had wanted to sleep with but would never dream of marrying, the penultimate girl, the one who came right before the ones they married. But it was no use mentioning that to Roger; she felt as sexy as a heap of rags.

"I've only had good sex with two people in my life," Roger had said. Was this meant as a consolation? And which two, she was *dying* to know! What about all those hookers? No, she wasn't going to ask, she couldn't bear to, she didn't think she could take it. Plus, she had this terrible feeling he would tell her. That day it was as if he was under oath on the witness stand: he would tell her anything, anything to be out of there, prove to her the marriage was over.

She hadn't dare ask in case one of them was that damn Jenny Sands. "That Jenny Sands was a *real* dish, and I mean *dish*—D-I-S-H!" Roger's mother had confided to her their first Christmas, as if this fact were somehow reassuring. The ghost of Jenny Sands hadn't bothered her until the day she'd uncovered that college picture of Roger and Jenny, looking impossibly young and fresh, straight out of some 1950s letter-sweater movie, Roger's short, slicked-back hair revealing boyishly sticking-out ears, but so happy, his arm wrapped around Jenny's shoulders, pulling her closer. It was winter, their cheeks were flushed, their noses bright, they were out-side—he had probably just come from the locker room after winning the Ivy League. Her yellow blond hair had been in the perfect flip that Lizzie had so admired in her extreme youth, hair like Shelley Fabares's or Millie the Model's. But Jenny hadn't just been a beautiful, fair-skinned blond; she'd also had those crinkly, sleepy eyes that looked so warm and full of love and vulnerable. Oh, dear God, all her life Lizzie'd wanted to be that girl look-ing out at her from under Roger's arm, *that* had been her ideal, not some screwed-up Radcliffe girl who talked too much! She had wanted to know everything there was to know about Jenny, but even that picture thrown so care-lessly at the bottom of a box in the basement hadn't prompted any reminiscences from Roger. "What's over is over," he'd said. She had shuddered then and she shud-dered now.

Then she learned about the affair. When on earth had he had *time* to have an affair? That had been the first thought that had crossed her mind. She needn't have worried because, merciful God, Roger was clearing his throat and taking a breath, suddenly in a rush to apprise her of all of the details. "Way back sometime in the fall," he said, sitting forward in his chair. All that time she thought he'd been adoring her, bragging about her new job in advertising. It flashed upon her the drunken night one of her advertising pals had said, "Wouldn't it be funny if Roger was playing around?" She'd laughed uproariously.

When had he had the affair, before or after their first anniversary? (Which, she thought to herself, was the same as asking before or after the flirting had started up for her. Had the affair pushed her to it subconsciously?) When, exactly when? she asked. But he couldn't remember, he was willing to try but he couldn't remember. *He couldn't remember?* He'd done something like that and he couldn't remember? Had he sat that night across from her on the first anniversary as an adulterer? To her, timing was everything.

Plus, she had always thought of him as so moral! She'd known he'd had a wild past, but that was when he was single. He was so upstanding in his work, where were those principles when it came to adultery? Hadn't he said once that, if he got married, he would never be unfaithful? And now he couldn't even remember *when* he'd taken the fatal plunge?

Why hadn't he admitted he'd had an affair in Carsy's office?

Well, he explained, he'd *wanted* to (Great! she thought, how comforting), but he just hadn't been able to bring himself to do it; he wasn't used to ever telling her how he really felt. (So we gather, she thought.) So who was it? Surely he remembered who it was. Well, it was that girl he'd told her about—she remembered the girl calling early in their romance and Roger taking the call in other room—it was the in-between girl, the girl he'd met years ago at Brandy's.

"How delightful you two were able to keep up, even after marriage," she couldn't resist saying. She remembered her because she had read the little flowery card that had been left in the kitchen a week or so after the phone call. It was a sin to read another person's mail—generally she wouldn't even open Roger's junk mail—but there it had been lying, so perfumedly, and so she had opened it: "I don't care if you are 'in love,'" it said, "you can come and visit me anytime." Jesus, who did she think she was, Mae West? But she certainly hadn't worried about her; at the time it had just made her feel smug. But why had Roger picked that particular girl when he'd had all those damn touchy-feely types at PRV just dying to be true to their feelings? Ask it all, ask anything; he was sitting there taking it, knowing when it was over, he was through. She couldn't say he was enjoying it, but why should he enjoy it? He said he didn't know; he just had. How long had it lasted, or was it still going on? It had ended sometime in the winter, he had ended it. When, exactly when? He tried to remember but shook his head. And why did he end it?

"All I know," he said, "was that I still loved you when I bought you that poker table for your birthday." How touching! So he had *still loved her* and gone and had an affair. Her mother had just happened to mention recently that some men just had affairs, that there were men who just had to, and their wives had to accept it. This was not the line she'd heard growing up. Was this what Roger was? She couldn't believe it.

He had still loved her in March then, so she wasn't all that crazy, but then he no longer loved her by April 20, when he walked out? Yes, she learned, she seemed to have gotten that right. What's more, he volunteered, he had never loved her the right way. Now he was volunteering stuff? She began to think she preferred to keep it at the question-and-answer grilling of the reluctant witness.

Did he have the affair maybe because she had decided not to have a baby? she asked, hopefully. Oh no, the last thing he'd wanted was a baby with her! Children, how was she supposed to take care of children if she couldn't open a can of tuna fish without almost bleeding to death? Or drive to work without half her dress dragging in the mud out the car door? The first night he'd *met* her, she'd had a wine stain running down the entire back of her dress. "Oh," she said, sunkenly, "I thought you loved me for that."

"I loved you for that wine stain," he said, "but I am also leaving you for that wine stain."

Was that his only affair, including that night after the merry-go-round bar?

"Yes," Roger said.

This was something, not much, but something, but then she ran out of questions she could bear to be answered. If only she could keep him there all day, but he was sitting dutifully, on the chair, not in the chair, ready, waiting to go. To think that once he had lived there, with her.

How was she going to stand the rest of the weekend, not even knowing where Roger was? Where would he be on Saturday night? she thought wildly. How could he be out in the world without her? Sunday, what would happen when she woke up Sunday? For some reason, she was showing a brave front, no tears, no tantrums, the good sport. Maybe because she knew it was useless, or maybe she was suddenly too wounded to respond. Probably though, it was because her hair was wet and bumping up in little hollow barrels where the rollers had been. She didn't know how vivid she wanted the scene to be when she remembered it over and over.

But now she had to let him go. She couldn't stand it, but the worst part was that she would simply have to

stand it. This happened to people all the time, people
with children—how did they stand it?

She looked achingly out the window at the Peugeot in
the driveway, next to the Subaru. She'd already had two
accidents in the driveway in the week since he'd left, both
at precisely 6 P.M. one day apart, though neither time had
she been in the car. The second time Hope and Leslie had
been in the car, heads poking through the open window,
as if to say, "Mama? Mama?" as the Subaru had rolled
down the driveway and across the busy street into the
side of a parked car. She'd rushed out shouting "I have
insurance, I have insurance!" to the little group of elderly
neighbors that had gathered, but they had just patted her
on the head and told her to take it easy. Everyone could
see, of course, that the Peugeot was no longer around.

18

The Parents Are Told

"It's in the genes," Roger's mother said to Lizzie over the phone. "It's good you're a nice, young, voluptuous thing because you'll find somebody else," and then she went on about her garden club. Transplanting rhododendrons? Lizzie was speechless. She'd naturally *assumed* Roger's mother would take up her cause as righteous, urge her son to return to his wife. Where were all those lectures on commitment now that she needed them? And where was old God these days, always being quoted left and right, well, bring Him on in! Surely this was the time to breathe some life into all those "Thou giveth unto's" etc., stuck into the corner of every mirror in his mother's house? While she certainly disapproved of her son's actions, Roger's mother seemed to accept them—almost clung to them—as an inevitability.

If it were in the genes, then the wives were blameless, of course. His mother's entire life had been built on the belief that a wife's duty was to husband and home. How could she bear to think that she, who had raked *all* the leaves and cooked every single meal and scraped the ice from her husband's windshield with her bare hands (not, she'd admitted to Lizzie, necessarily very *agreeably*), how could she bear that after all of that, *she* had driven away her husband? Well, in fact, she had; it may not have been her fault exactly, but she had. And so, Lizzie supposed, had she herself. The difference was that Lizzie wanted to find out why, whereas Roger's mother was too terrified even to wonder. "Well, dear girl, I will pray for you," Roger's mother had said at the end of her monologue, and that had been that.

As for Roger's father, well, she'd figured his father probably wouldn't even call, though she knew he loved her, because he so adored his son. She had never known a parent to admire a child in such an unqualified way. Even his senior year at Dartmouth, after Roger'd woken himself up out of a drunken stupor by totaling his father's car into a stone wall, and later the same week had been thrown in jail for breaking off tombstones, not a word of criticism had come from Mr. Stoner, who had driven all night up to Hanover to speak on his behalf in court. Just: "Rog, they say things come in threes; let's prove them wrong." No, his father would be sorry, she'd thought, but he wouldn't call. But Roger's father *had* called her up, right away, after putting down the phone from Roger, and asked, "Is there a third party?"

"No," she'd said. No, Roger wasn't even in love with someone else; he evidently just couldn't stand being with her! Really, when she thought about it, it was so much worse this way and more embarrassing. But Roger's father had sounded so relieved, saying Roger just couldn't walk out on a marriage so soon, he would keep talking to him and that she should call him (Roger's father) anytime, every night if she wanted, collect.

Oh, those phone calls to Roger's father! She would come home from a movie she'd been too jumpy to sit through and race up the outside stairway and into the apartment and start dialing the number before she could catch her breath. The sound of his voice was sometimes the only thing that brought her any relief, however temporary, and, she hoped, she suspected her voice did the same for him.

Her parents were updated with the news. "That's a hell of a note," her father said, shaking his head, and wondering why a man would ever choose the life of a lonely bachelor.

Roger had stopped going to Carsy—he'd only gone because she'd made him. Oh God, what a great idea that had been. Carsy had done nothing but give Roger a sound pat on the back for leaving her, and sent him on his way. *She*, of course, still went to Carsy, even though she hated his guts. She had no choice. She couldn't eat or sleep and spent her nights roaming the streets of Cambridge in the Subaru, as if she might happen upon Roger lost in the wilds.

It was her second session, when, before Carsy got a chance to bring up sex, she volleyed up what she hoped was a wounding sarcasm. "I just want to thank you for working so hard to keep the marriage together," she said.

"Face it," he replied, "the marriage is over."

"How can you say that? You don't even *know* us!" she shouted, but as it turned out, it was the nicest possible thing he could have said to her, because suddenly all the anxiety vanished. She felt, if not exactly happy, normal again. It seemed it wasn't the abandonment itself that was keeping her awake all night, but the *fear* of abandonment. Once she faced the fact that Roger had left, the crippling terror was gone. Her relief, however, was dampened by some specifics from Carsy that she could have lived contentedly her whole life without. "Did you think sex with Roger was good?" asked Dr. Carsy.

"Yes!" she said violently. She wouldn't have dreamed

of thinking otherwise, let alone admitting otherwise—
even if it were true. It was so disloyal! Of course, it *was*
true; their sex life hadn't been good for many months.
After they'd gotten married sex had seemed, well, almost
incestuous. But any beginning social worker could have
told you that was a symptom, not a cause.

"You see," Carsy explained gravely, "Roger never
had good sexual relations with you."

"Never?" she said. "*Never?*"

"The first time you had relations, Roger didn't climax," Carsy announced a little too triumphantly.

She was beginning to think they were having a little
problem with semantics here, or had Roger declined to
share with Dr. Carsy what they'd done on the banks of
the reservoir that first night? She suspected Roger of a little cheating here in not counting that encounter as technically making love. For a moment she was tempted to
bring in some crude words, because she always loved it
when the shrinks suddenly took on your lingo, something
evidently taught in shrink school: "So when you were
really 'pissed off' at your brother . . . " they would say in
their stilted effort to speak "the patient's language."
Unfortunately, she just couldn't talk about sex; she was a
WASP and it wasn't in the manual. "It's all right what a
person does, as long as he does it behind closed doors,"
she could hear her great-aunt Elizabeth saying. Plus her
mother had taught her that people who had to talk about
their sex lives weren't having a good time. She had to let
Carsy win that round.

She began seeing Carsy every Tuesday in his office at
Brookhill, driving up the long, curving driveway on her
lunchbreak, delivering to Carsy one afternoon the huge
packet of letters she'd been writing Roger daily since he'd
walked out. Oh, the theories that had poured out of her
at two in the morning when she hadn't been able to

sleep! How Roger had learned to shut off his emotions when he was twelve years old, after the evening he'd realized Mrs. Ash was the woman his father loved. How when the least problem arose in Roger's own marriage, he had been so terrified that he, too, would be trapped in a loveless marriage, that he'd had to leave! How Roger hadn't had "the mechanics" to talk about problems, having never seen his parents talk about anything, let alone fight! Then: How about, he had something where he wanted to prove he was as bad as his father? And so forth and so forth. You could go on forever with these psychological theories, that she knew, and sound very learned, in a talk-radio sort of way. No need to make clear to Roger, the babe in the woods here, how you could explain two exactly opposite phenomena with the same psychological theory.

Roger had loved the letters; she'd had to pry them away from him to bring them in to Carsy, and even he was softened by them. Well, she was a great shrink; with her family she'd had a lot of training. Still, she was a bit sorry for poor Carsy, having to read those manic illegible scribbles, written late at night without her lenses in.

"I can't be married to a saint" had been her favorite line from one (of the two) of Roger's brief missives back. A saint! The girl who'd come back to her husband one night with all the buttons of her overcoat torn off?

The Watertown house had sold the first week it was on the market, but by the time the closing date came, with Roger gone a month, the grass was so long it was going to seed. It killed him to see the house so neglected; Lizzie had actually said she suspected the reason he'd come over one Saturday "to work on the marriage" was really "to work on the front steps." Well, who else was going to finish the cementing? Not that that was why

he'd come. He supposed it was to prove that the marriage was over. He didn't know, really. He just knew that
he was going crazy trying to arrange closings on two
houses he didn't live in or expect to live in. The buyers,
said the real estate agent to Roger on phone, wouldn't
pass papers until Roger mowed the lawn.

"Tell them to buy a fucking cow and have him chew
it!" Roger had yelled over the phone. He had been tight
all week, running around trying to get a mortgage,
which, because of some new law in Boston, couldn't be
obtained unless the lead paint was first removed. How
were you supposed to get the lead paint scraped off if
you didn't have the mortgage that allowed you to own
the house? Roger wanted to know. No one could answer:
not the loan officer, not the loan officer's superior, not
some goddamn vice president. Luckily, thanks to Lizzie's
Saks bill, Roger and she were in enough debt to be given
an enormous swing loan to buy the town house before
they got the mortgage. Then Roger'd had to find lead
paint scrapers plus a floor guy who would come in and
sand the floors over the Fourth of July weekend plus
spread two coats of polyurethane. (Roger would do the
third, and a fourth on the front hall.) After numerous
phone calls, he orchestrated it so that Lizzie could go up
to Maine with William that Friday and come down Monday night when he would have the furniture and boxes
already moved in. Finally he had it all worked out for
her.

Why were they even buying the town house? she'd
asked Carsy. Could it be that *that* was the whole problem, Roger's not wanting to sell his house, his first house
that he'd worked so hard on? These theories, they were
driving her nuts. When were they going to stop obsessing
her? No, said Carsy, buy the house, Roger seemed to

want to buy the house. Why does he want to buy the house? she asked. What is it, my buy-off gift? Carsy couldn't say. Go ahead and buy the house, repeated Carsy, just as he had said, keep working! when early on she had wanted to quit her job to work on the relationship.

She supposed the job had saved her. She'd come a long way from the campaign for the King's Department Store merger when she'd written the little poem about princes and princesses (representing the smaller stores that were being merged) turning into kings, and actually (though she'd been a bit nervous about those prin*cesses* turning into kings) shown it with bashful pride to the head copywriter. Now she'd been given an opportunity to do a whole campaign from the beginning for the new fast-food restaurant at which the hamburgers were half price, the only problem being they were also a quarter the size. Poor food for poor people had been her first thought, but the theory from the creative director was to talk about price, no need to mention size—that would become apparent soon enough. She had written a bunch of ads, then waltzed into the board of directors' meeting of the large corporation that owned the chain, and made an impromptu, sterling speech, suddenly discovering an ever-increasing brilliance in the campaign as each word fell from her mouth. "There are *four* reasons why this campaign is the only way to go . . . " she began, not having the slightest notion what one reason was, let alone four, but as it happened, it didn't matter. "Number one" she said with authority, and lo and behold, out came a reason, and a rather compelling one, at that—why hadn't she thought of that one before? "Number two," she continued, with a dramatic pause, before the next reason, even more compelling, rolled off her silver tongue and around the hearts of the gentlemen of the board. She was a great success! That night, as her boss congratulated her while she was pounding away on the typewriter about french fries, she solemnly said, "Work is my life."

The packing up of the wedding presents and so forth for the big move, she had to admit, wasn't a barrel of fun, but when Roger came over that Friday before the Fourth of July weekend to help get things organized for the hippie movers (whom he'd found from some ad in the *Phoenix*), there was a little of the festive feeling before a move. Roger had everything taken care of, he said, they were sanding the town house floors as they spoke, all should be done by Monday night when she came back from Maine. Roger had quite the list of things to tell her. He'd made himself a copy of the key, he said, did she mind? He wouldn't use it without letting her know. He'd bought her a little black-and-white TV, as their old black and white had been dead for months. And a bright, spanking-new toaster oven. (The kitchen was a butler's pantry and had no oven.) What next, was he going to carry her over the threshold, the blushing divor-cée? Why was he still taking care of her? she couldn't help thinking. It didn't matter that the floors were being done, who cared? They were breaking up! Then she hap-pened to say, out of the blue, as she still could not stop the steady stream of pop psychology coursing through her brain: "Maybe you're mad at your mother; she's the saint, if there has to be a saint around here." Who knew, she was just trying it out for something to say, but there, suddenly, was Roger bursting into tears. What had she said? She'd just been sort of casually analyzing. She hadn't *meant* anything of any great importance, she probably hadn't even meant what she said. What *had* she said, anyway? *She* certainly hadn't been paying much attention. But here was Roger, not a drop from those ice-blue eyes for two straight months, but now here he was welling up and pouring out the tears, wailing like a baby, saying over and over, "Maybe I *do* love you, maybe I *do!*"

What was a girl to make of this? After spending the entire week packing up their wedding presents, their wedding pictures, their books, the photo of the two of them the summer before they were married sitting on the deck in Maine, arms draped around each other ("Jungle Love" Aunt Cornelia had captioned it)—a week of drinking wine and bemoaning her lost youth—after all of this "healing process," suddenly Roger, after drumming and drumming into her thick skull that he had never even been *attracted* to her, comes up with, Know what? maybe I *do* love you.

She let Roger have his little cry while she patted his back, her head beginning to throb as his tears turned into happy sniffles. Now he was smiling and crying and hugging her with these sappy eyes, so unlike Roger it was making her just a little uncomfortable, and then, mercifully, William came to pick her up to drive her to Maine.

"So, see you Monday!" Roger yelled gaily after them, and they drove off, leaving Roger, phoneless, to wait for the hippie movers, sitting merrily on a box of wedding china.

19

The Simple Life

It had all been so confusing for so long. He'd made a mess of things—he didn't think there'd be much disagreement from all sides on that—but he'd honestly believed that he didn't love Lizzie, maybe never had. But, either *adding* to the confusion or *clearing up* the confusion, it was now evident that he *did* love Lizzie, and therefore, it followed (didn't it?) that he wanted to stay with Lizzie. He just needed a little more time. A little more time to sort himself out, to ease into being with Lizzie again. And so, with "The Cafe" off the air for July and August, he decided to move up to Maine for the summer (with Lizzie coming up weekends), to fulfill his dream of living in a cabin in the woods, with the birds and the trees and the trips to the Lumber Barn, where life was as calm as the deep black lake.

The simple life: no television, no dry cleaning to pick up, just he and his toolbox, for six whole weeks—a lifetime! Lizzie had always joked that he would get half a project done (half the roof shingled, half the wall up in the bathroom, and so on), and then move on to a new one, so that if you had the imagination, you could envision the whole thing done. But really, he had just been frustrated that there was not more time. Dutifully, the winter before, he had waited until 7 A.M. on a Sunday before hitting the first nail of the day. Then he'd ventured a tentative tap-tap, then paused, until, confident he had tested the water sufficiently, bang bang bang! and he'd been off and running until nightfall. Now there was nothing in his way. He could saw and hammer and stuff insulation from dawn until dark, to his heart's content.

Instead, he awakened on clear summer mornings to the sparkling lake and chirping birds with a horrible panic clutching his chest so that he was literally panting for breath, stumbling about the cabin, looking for a pair of pants to pull on, trying to get some cereal down his clogged throat, until he remembered with relief that he needed some two-by-two tubing. Might as well give Winter's Hardware in Watertown the business, he'd think to himself, because Winter's was cheaper than the Lumber Barn, and off he'd hop in his car to drive down to Watertown and back up again, a four-hour trip he joyfully undertook that summer, almost on a daily basis.

All his life there had never been enough time in the day to get the thousandth thing done, but now, when it was the last thing he needed on earth, Roger had all the time in the world, limitless, interminable time, not even a phone call to interrupt him, four acres and four shacks to work on, and he was too screwed-up to get a single thing done. He had completely lost the concentration that had once allowed him to blissfully lose himself in his work, and in its place was a dull, sick throbbing, as if a plate had been inserted in his brain, and a fluttering queerness in his heart. But the drive to Watertown and back gave him a feeling of accomplishment without taxing his mental powers. He'd smoke a joint; pretend he was a hippie.

One time he saw a bunch of hippies in an old pickup truck and pulled up beside their opened window and passed them a joint, driving sixty miles an hour down Route 95. For a brief moment, he'd been filled with joy! "I'm a hippie; you're a hippie!" he'd felt like shouting out. Back and forth all summer he would drive. Drive up, drive down, any excuse.

The arrangement was, he would do projects all week long in Maine, and Lizzie would join him on the weekends, which, frankly, was about all he could take. He was always glad to see Lizzie on a Friday night, glad they were planning to stay together, but by the end of the weekend he couldn't wait to drive her over to Portland to put her on the bus back to Boston. The tightness he felt during the week was nothing compared to the turmoil he felt when Lizzie was there. It was compounded by the fact that he had to pretend everything was fine, that it was great they were staying together, that none of what had happened had happened. How could he let Lizzie know the confusion churning inside? He couldn't imagine telling her that, after all he'd put her through, he still had doubts. Not that he could have articulated his doubts if he'd wanted to, except for the most terrible one, which he could never tell her: that though he loved her, he no longer desired her sexually. So he masked his misery, and she let him, because he sensed she didn't really want to see.

The sense of relief he would feel as he bundled her off onto the bus! It lasted a good thirty minutes, until he'd driven back and faced the empty cabin alone.

Taking the bus had seemed much simpler than driving up to the cabin by herself, having to take all those turns off the highway and to have the toll money ready and to worry about how to get off Route 95. No, thank you.

The bus was so nice, sort of ethereal, sitting up so high and looking out that picture-window front windshield, boasting the blue-tinted panoramic view of the highway, as they rode serenely above all the squabbling cars. She always sat near the front, giving her the feeling that the bus driver was personally taking such good care of her ("And leave the driving to us!" had promised, so correctly, the commercial in her youth). The bus station in Boston *was* a bit depressing, but she'd just jump in a cab home to the house on Marlboro Street, turn on all the lights to make it cozy, then turn them all off and go straight to bed.

She felt like a little girl giddy and drained from having to act grown-up all day; she never wanted to think another grown-up thought about life as long as she lived. Fortunately, things had settled down since the Monday Roger had moved her in. The hippie movers, it turned out, had arrived twenty-four hours late and then stolen Roger's leather vest—she wondered how much Roger was liking hippies these days. Roger had spent that whole weekend working industriously on the move, while she'd basked in Maine sunlight, listening to William groaning from eating too many Fritos, then to his defeated "Why not?" as he'd helped himself to some cake. That night, writhing on the couch, William had been forced, not without bitterness, to phone his girlfriend long distance for the sympathy he had not received from Lizzie. Meanwhile, Roger was gaily lifting huge boxes around the various crouching configurations of people scraping lead paint and sanding floors, carrying all the furniture upstairs into the master bedroom, the one room where the polyurethane was dry, then setting up the rickety little child's cot his mother had bought years ago to martyr herself with in his attic (or so she'd hoped) when she visited, the perfect size for a (short) seven-year-old. He'd even somehow managed to get the cover on the queen-size duvet, which engulfed the cot to the point of toppling it over. Then, he'd rushed out to fight his way through the Independence Day Sale crowds at Lechmere's to buy a *second* toaster oven. "And, I got you two forks and a knife!" he'd said excitedly that Monday night when she'd returned from Maine.

"But tell me you're someday going to live here!" she'd said. "Yes, yes," he'd agreed, kissed her, and left, giving her some happiness that night as Hope and Leslie, eyeing the shrunken bed, had gingerly arranged themselves on the overflowing eiderdown, and she'd drifted, exhausted, off to sleep. What she was exhausted from she couldn't say, having done absolutely nothing all weekend—possibly it was the sight of all Roger had accomplished. The next morning, however, was less than placid when she awoke and couldn't find the toothpaste or the hair dryer or the damn tin forks, and hating Roger for it; then losing Hope, who had spent the first half of their jog being lured stupidly into the smelly river by a duck and the second half rolling sensuously in something dead on the banks, and hating Roger for it. How could Hope ever find her way home to a new house? What am I going to do? she'd thought fiercely to herself, walking back from the jog, I hate him! I hate him!, and then when she'd opened the door of the town house, there had been Hope panting happily away, like some damn thing from *The Incredible Journey*, having linked up with one of the guys who was renting the upstairs apartment.

And then had begun the weekends of visiting Roger in Maine, and the Sunday nights, after Roger had dropped her off, of reading *Poldark* all the way home in the bus, in the taxi, in bed until she went to sleep. Even after Roger had announced he wanted to stay married, the only thing that blanked her mind and restored her

calm was reading about the woes of Poldark. Never
before had she read trash; she'd simply read the good
stuff as if it were trash, to see if they got married in the
end—three times she had read *War and Peace*, and never
so much as grazed a line of war. All her life she had
breezed through great works of literature in this fashion,
it never bothering her when she missed characterization
or couldn't follow the plot, but after Roger left her, she
had been unable to read a word of anything, until she'd
happened one day in the drugstore upon the Poldark
series, a flimsy line of paperbacks that she suspected (but
decided not to investigate) had been written *after* the
popular television series had run.

It hadn't been an easy summer—Roger still looked
troubled, racked by guilt for having walked out on her,
she supposed—but in their own little way they had been
happy, working things out. She was supremely confident.
She knew he loved her now, and love to her was a sanc-
tuary that admitted no doubt—though once she had
found herself saying to Roger out of the blue, "You
know, if you ever walk out again, that's it."

"Absolutely," Roger had said, he would never leave
her again. The Friday her vacation began, Roger (who it
seemed had been on vacation all summer) drove down
from Maine to bring her back up, with a brief stop at
Firestone and Parson to buy a brand-new wedding ring.

"What date would you like inscribed on it?" the
gray-haired gentleman had asked.

"Oh, I don't know," she had said to Roger. "What do
you think?"

"I don't know," Roger had said. "What about
today?" And they'd laughed. They were so happy.

He was always hoping there was going to be some
solution, some course of action that would make him feel

better. First he had thought it was breaking up with
Lizzie; then, realizing that he still loved her, he'd thought
deciding to stay with her would be the answer. But he'd
still felt tight. Then there was the scheme to live in Maine
the rest of the summer, but all he seemed to accomplish
was driving Lizzie to and from the bus station in Portland. He had plenty of energy, but he just couldn't seem
to put it into anything but wanting to explode. He
remembered Harry saying one weekend the year before
as he watched Roger sheetrock (half) the ceiling in the
cabin bathroom, "If only I could find a way to market
Roger's energy!" Now the only damn thing he'd gotten
done all summer was whittling a wedge of log into a
birdhouse. His cousin Sophie had come up with her family one weekend and said it looked like the Trenton State
Prison. He'd actually had his feelings hurt, and over an
ugly birdhouse. That weekend to the laughter of all (but
his) he'd stuck it on a pole and poured birdseed in it, but
before he'd even finished *filling it*, chipmunks were there
sucking it up, breaking off the neat little perches he'd
screwed in where the birds were supposed to stand.

Plus, with all summer to sort out his feelings, he still
hadn't resolved anything. He'd said to himself, Okay I've
got all the time in the world, let's figure things out. Surely
I can figure things out. One plus two equals three. I love
Lizzie and she loves me, therefore we should be able to
stay together. But do I love her the right way? Is she the
right person? Who is the right person? Jenny Sands (the
blond with the big breasts), Lizzie (the wife with the big
breasts), or Jean Stock (the hippie with the big breasts)?
But the only thing he'd been able to figure out was that
he liked big breasts.

Then he'd bought Lizzie the ring. He had done it to
make her happy, of this he was certain, so why on the
way to Maine for her two-week vacation had he started

feeling like he couldn't breathe again? Maybe, he ventured to himself, the problem was that he hadn't told her all of the truth. Maybe a little confession would help? He didn't know. All his life he had found lying about personal things was always easier than telling the truth, at least with women. (With men it didn't matter; you didn't have to have relationships with men, only women seemed to want them.) Of course, he supposed he was thinking mostly of his mother, to whom he had never said an honest word, not wanting to upset her. She had always gone on about how difficult everything had been—"No one ever had it more difficult than I taking care of two little boys and mixing the yellow into the margarine"—and how she had had to take out the garbage herself, and how little Roger's father had done. Really, he supposed, what she'd been complaining about was the one thing she couldn't change, nobody could change—how Roger's father felt about her. Well, Roger's role in his eyes had been to do as little as possible to upset her—or rather to be careful not to let her know about the things he did that would upset her.

Even when his mother had *known* he was lying, though, as she had the time he'd thrown up all over the rug at age fifteen after his father's Yale reunion and blamed it on Chip Benson who had been visiting from Exeter (but was by then safely back within its confines), even when she'd said, "I know it was you and not Chip Benson who threw up on the rug." Nevertheless, she'd walked away. He hadn't had to tell her, Yes, Mother, I drink beer, and when possible, I drink it until I'm sick as a dog. He hadn't had to talk about it. It didn't even matter that she knew the truth; he'd been spared the confrontation.

Lying was always his first instinct. Lying about little things was something of a game, you also had to know how to disarm with the truth, when necessary. Usually when a cop stopped him for speeding he said, "Yes, sir, you're right. I was speeding, and there is absolutely no excuse," and, undeservedly, he would get off. Of course sometimes he outsmarted himself. Like the time the winter before when he'd almost gone to jail because a cop had stopped him in a crime-ridden part of Boston near PRV and by mistake Roger'd absentmindedly handed him the fake I.D. he'd had made up so he could get a dump sticker at the town one over in Maine that didn't make you recycle. The worst part, he supposed, was that he'd used the name of this really nice guy in the next town who'd recently died. At any rate, the next thing he'd known, the cop was coming back from his car with his gun drawn, and throwing Roger up against the side of a wall to pat him down, right off the parkway near PRV, a curious scene for any of his colleagues to view driving home from work. Roger had immediately told the cop the whole true story of the dump.

"Well," the cop had said to Roger against the wall, "I *should* be taking you in."

"Sir, all you'd be bringing in would be an asshole," Roger had said, and they'd parted, the best of friends.

Now in the car on the way to Maine with Lizzie, he was feeling tight again. Okay, he thought, try the truth for a change, confess to Lizzie.

"That night," he said as he swerved into the hairpin turn connecting Route 95 to Route 1, "I didn't tell you the truth about that night. I *was* with Jean Stock."

She was crying so hard he had to pull over in the middle of the exit ramp. She ran out of the car and up the hill crazily, toward the parking lot of the HoJo's motel court. He ran after her, saying he was sorry, he couldn't stand to hurt her, he would never hurt her ever again, please, please, he was so sorry, he would *never* hurt her again.

"Were you in love with her?" she sobbed.

"No, no," he insisted.

"Was she in love with you?"

Tell the truth, he said to himself. "Yes, or anyway she said she was."

"She did, did she? She was just dying to get you in the old sack ever since that basketball game."

What basketball game? he thought.

"Actually," he said (be honest!), "I had to persuade her I was separated."

"Oh, right!" she said. "What does she have, small breasts?"

"Not necessarily," he said. Oh, what could he say to make her feel better? He racked his brain frantically. "When I told her I wasn't going to see her anymore, she said she was behind us one hundred percent!" he tried brightly.

"Oh," said Lizzie, "fuck *her!*"

20

The Tide Turns

Oh why had he told her! She didn't want to know! Now
she would have to live with it forever, until the day she
died. She had been *so willing* to believe otherwise, in the
face of all facts to the contrary, why couldn't he have left
well enough alone? If he had just gone to a decent haircut-
ter instead of those $6-cut places he was so proud of, he
would have seen the covers of the magazines: "Why You
Should *Not* Tell Your Wife About the Other Woman."
Now what was she supposed to do with this tasty piece of
information? Did it make her feel any better? Hadn't she
gotten enough of the gist when he'd walked out on her
and sent along the message, kindness of Carsy, that he had
never enjoyed sex with her? Well, at least *he* was happy
now, she guessed *that* had been the point. There he was,
humming around the cabin, lighting the match to the hot
water heater, turning on the old, giant camp icebox, oh, he
couldn't be happier. She loved him, but she had to say she
didn't know if loving him made it worth knowing about
Jean Stock.

All those weeks of holding hands and working at

staying together! He was not a man who had had *one* affair, but a man who had *affairs*. She was beginning to wonder if all men had affairs. How had her parents found each other? Here she was with a man who, moments after crying to her for help, had dropped her home and blithely gone off to sleep with another girl, while she stayed up all night like an ass writing long ana- lytical letters about his childhood—it just wasn't the way she had expected life to be! Suddenly, now, on their first real day back together, all the ardor to save Roger that had driven her for so many weeks was gone. She won- dered if she'd ever feel the same about anything again.

She doesn't hate me! Roger thought joyfully to him- self. He had told her about Jean Stock, and the world hadn't come to a halt! He'd never said anything like this to anyone, but now he'd said it, and nothing horrible had happened. She was even making jokes as they were unpacking in the cabin—well, not jokes, she never even *got* jokes, let alone made them, but she was being funny in that way that never translated, but was funnier than jokes. At one point he had had to sit down, he was laughing so hard. He felt warm inside. He thought to himself, I really like this girl, I really like her so much.

Then, over the next two weeks, everybody, but every- body came up to visit them in Maine. Their friends, her parents, his mother and aunt, his father and his wife. Earlier his father had told him that the whole episode of his walking out on Lizzie had been so upsetting he'd even thought about it on the golf course in the middle of his backswing. His father had always phoned every few weeks—he knew how much he meant to his father—but that summer when he had called he'd wanted to *talk about things*. He'd never talked to his father, except on safe topics like politics or sports; he had felt so embarrassed when his father had ventured forth on the subject of Roger's marriage problems, he hadn't known how to answer. "No man is an island, Rog," his father had said. "Yes sir, Dad," Roger had replied. Sir! He'd never called his father "sir" in his life!

But now his father and Mrs. Ash were up for a triumphant visit. As they were leaving he heard him say to Lizzie, "Well, I can see that things are better than ever."

But when no one was around she would see him outside looking so miserable. They had talks, and he cried a lot, but she couldn't seem to lighten his load. She had to forgive him Jean Stock, almost immediately, without so much as a recriminating word. As the days passed, she couldn't even bring up his infidelity—it would have been like tossing a cinder block to a drowning man. Instead he would come to her looking so wretched, and she would put down whatever she was doing and hold him while they had a good cry (now that she had Jean Stock, she found it quite easy to join in on the tears), and she'd think, *great*, and then peer out the window half an hour later and see him sitting slumped on a rock, looking as miserable as before. He loved her, she knew that, and yet for the first time it was occurring to her that loving someone wasn't enough. He'd loved her when he'd slept with Jean Stock, and he'd loved her when he'd first walked out. She had always looked to love as the be-all and end-all; it had never occurred to her that love wasn't simple, that anything could be as complex as it appeared to be with Roger. Not with her: she was all one way or another, a simple girl, in these matters, anyway. Either you loved someone or you didn't. She didn't understand Roger; oh, rationally, she was sure if she kept chipping away, someday she might intellectually understand, but in her gut, she didn't get it.

She had never understood Harry and all his depressions and crazy states, and yet she'd stood by him, through it all, a mess herself but when it came to her brother, a rock of Gibraltar. It was in her blood: in her family you were either crazy or built to support those who were (or both, like her mother). Had she married Roger because subconsciously she had sensed he was a wreck down deep and needed her? She would like to have given herself credit, but she knew she had married Roger because she was going to get married that year, and he was the one who asked. Not that she hadn't been madly in love with him (she would never forget the piercing joy of their first fall together), but she might have been madly in love with someone else: such was her capacity and her downfall. She shuddered to think whom she might have married; then of course, she shuddered to think whom she *had* married. And, she figured, while with Harry what she had tried to save him from had been himself; with Roger she got the sneaky feeling that what she was saving him from was *herself*—a dawning realization that understandably tended to take a bit of her missionary fervor away.

And yet, in addition to loving him desperately, she *liked* Roger so much, she really did, and while the marriage hadn't been so great, now after what they'd been through it had so much more potential, now she knew more of who he was.

But this working on the marriage! She was exhausted. Still, exhaustion was not what made her feel dead inside. Jean Stock made her feel dead inside. She had always thought she was so jaded. She hadn't even known how innocent she was, until she lost that innocence with a single sentence about Jean Stock. Meanwhile, of course, Roger himself was brimming with self-discovery.

How excited he had been the other day when he had

actually remembered a dream. The only time he'd ever
told her a dream it was about how he'd ordered a beer
for eleven dollars and it had been warm. But this dream,
he couldn't wait to relate it to her: He had called up
Jenny Sands. (She was getting a little sick of Jenny Sands,
if anyone wanted to know.) "I wondered how long it
would take before you called," Jenny had said over the
phone. When he'd got there all kinds of guys were hanging around, presumably her boyfriends, about to go up
to Maine, who'd said to Roger, want to come? Sure,
Roger had said, it sounded good to him—he seemed to
bear no animosity toward the group of boyfriends—but,
he explained, he had to run some errands first. Then he'd
gone out and gotten an incredibly short haircut, after
which he'd looked at his watch (which in real life he
never wore, because he hated to think time was elapsing)
and said, "Jeez, it's five-thirty. I've got to report to jail."
Evidently he'd been out on some furlough, and the next
thing he knew he was reporting to jail thinking better
ring Jenny and tell her he wouldn't be able to come back
because he was in jail.

"So, that's the dream!" he'd said proudly to Lizzie,
who for a second had felt relieved about the lack of passion evinced for Jenny in the dream. But then it had hit
her.

"I suppose jail represents our marriage?" she'd said.

"Gee," Roger had said excitedly, "I never thought of
that!"

The truth was, she wasn't sure how much she would
want to know about Roger's life, should at some future
date it exclude her. The more she knew him, the more she
loved him, and the more she realized that she could not
bear to be his friend if she was not his wife.

After a few days at Dixwell Notch, they'd dashed
back to the cabin and Hope and Leslie. When that didn't

seem to make them any happier, they'd rushed off to the Cranberry Hill Inn for lunch.

All the way there she kept talking about Roger getting a wedding ring, too. She'd been brought up by her father to think two-ring ceremonies were tacky. Of course, since almost everything was tacky to her father and his family, it was hard to keep up. At their wedding rehearsal, for instance, her father and his sister had been horrified at the thought of Roger and Lizzie kissing at the altar—her parents, it seemed, had merely smiled at each other—but then Roger had said, "Either I kiss your daughter at the altar or I don't marry her," and that had been that. Still, up to this very moment she, too, had been guilty of a prejudice against two-ring ceremonies, but now she strongly supported the concept. Why shouldn't the man wear a ring to let other people (like, for instance, Jean Stock) know right off the bat that he was off bounds? If the girl wore a ring, why shouldn't the boy wear a ring? And yet for some reason Roger wouldn't agree.

They pulled into the Cranberry Hill Inn parking lot, but Roger made no move to get out.

"It's just that I don't feel the same way, I mean, I don't feel the same intimacy with you I felt with Jenny Sands," he said to his lap.

"You know," she said—she was thinking fast, she was good at this—"I know *just* what you mean. I felt exactly the same way with Richard Townsend. It's never the same as it is with your first love."

"It isn't, it isn't?" he cried out. Suddenly he looked so relieved! Pity, really, that she was making the whole thing up. Try as she might, she couldn't actually remember what it had felt like having sex with Richard Townsend. After two straight months of wandering the campus quoting "Though nothing can bring back the hour of splendor in the grass, of glory in the flower . . . " she'd gotten over him, wiped him clean off the slate. No, she couldn't recall a thing.

"Nothing ever is the same as first love," she continued solemnly, elaborating, prevaricatingly, that the way she had felt about Richard sexually she would never feel again with anybody, and yet (oh, she was good!) she could never have married him.

"Yes!" said Roger ecstatically, if he'd married Jenny he'd be divorced now, too! He looked into her eyes, tears brimming.

Intimacy, there was a new one for him, but he couldn't quite say "sex"; as it was, he couldn't *believe* he was actually saying what he was saying. He had never spoken like this to anyone in his life. He had told her to her face that he didn't like having sex with her! And now all he wanted was to get back to the cabin and have sex with her!

They raced back to the cabin and made love three times. He had never been happier.

Certainly she was glad he'd ripped off her clothes—God, she had kept herself from this thought, but it was true: Sex with Roger had become something to be dreaded since he had walked out. On the one hand, Carsy had told her that Roger had complained that she was so outrageous, why wasn't she outrageous in bed. On the other hand, she'd kept wondering how was she to begin the things (whatever they were) to *be* so outrageous if whenever she touched him, he sort of jumped? Now, after their little discussion at the Cranberry Hill Inn parking lot, he was all mad for her, thrilled with his passion, but quite frankly, except for the feeling, what had been outrageous? Really, it was the same old stuff

from *The Sensuous Woman* that it had always been,
which, let it be said, had always been great with her.
Well, now she could relax a little and not have to keep
listening to that Meatloaf song, "Two Out of Three Ain't
Bad" and get a tiny lump in her throat. It was a great end
to the vacation. Let him go back to PRV and see Jean
Stock in the halls; he was hers.

Two weeks later they were back in Boston celebrating
Roger's birthday. He cried during the dinner she'd made
him, he was so touched by all the little things she had
done. "Aren't you glad you're with me on your birthday,
that next year you won't have to turn thirty-five alone?"
she'd said, and he'd burst out again. She was used to his
crying now; he was always crying, although not as much
as he had in Maine. Actually, by his birthday he'd gone a
couple of days without wrenching tears, which always
worried her. He pretty much wavered these days between
being really tense or crying so hard he couldn't catch his
breath—you took what you got. When she wasn't with
him she could always gloss over that part a bit and think
how glad she was that she had a husband. She would
walk home from work behind Deborah, another copywriter, single, who at thirty had just bought herself a studio condominium, and think to herself how she, Lizzie,
was *so* lucky not to be alone.

Things seemed to be going well: They'd been back in
Boston ten days and had only had one fight. Well, not a
fight really, in that Roger's only participation had been to
gently try to fend her off while she punched his stomach.
She'd been in such a good mood that evening, all dressed
up in designer jeans to go sit in the bar at "The Cafe" its
first night back on the air. But when she'd arrived at PRV
she'd come across a girl who had been signing out, a
plain-faced girl, but tall and thin with long, straight
dirty-blond hair, in corduroys and work boots, and sud-

denly she knew that this was Jean Stock. She looked her once in the face; the girl startled and scurried out. She checked the sign-out sheet. There it was: *Jean Stock.* The behind-you-one-hundred-percent girl herself.

A few days after the birthday dinner she told Roger that her favorite cousin, Merry, was coming for the weekend. ("Do you know what it's *like* to go through life named Merry," Merry had once said to her gloomily. Merry had started out very social, a wearer of charm bracelets and a player of tennis at the country club, and was now living alone in the mountains with a cat and no plumbing, happy as could be.) "Great," Roger had said, though for a moment he had looked distracted. She guessed he wanted to spend the weekend alone with her, get some more sobbing in, but what could she do? He was looking kind of tense again, too, well, he was due for a good downpour. She hoped they could get it in before Saturday morning, when Merry was arriving.

That Friday night Spencer's wife, Cecelia, called her. Cecelia was a delicate-looking redhead Spencer had met on a meditation retreat and married a couple of months after Lizzie and Roger's wedding. (Harry had gotten married that year, too; it was a competitive family.) There had been this little period after Spencer's engagement when the engagement was off—she remembered asking Spencer about it one night in Maine while Cecelia dozed on his arm and Spencer had said, shh, shhh—but then whatever had been the problem had gone away, she supposed, and they'd gotten married and moved to California, where Spencer had segued from teaching meditation to becoming a stockbroker, making more than $100,000 a year. Their father said he wanted Spencer to write a book: *From Marijuana to Merrill Lynch.* Cecelia was a quiet girl, so quiet that when you turned to ask her what she thought of a movie, she would smile in varying degrees, as if you were supposed to translate a tiny upward movement of the lips into, okay, but not great. Beautiful and silent: everything that Spencer had hoped and dreamed for his own sister but that Lizzie had failed so miserably at achieving. Probably Cecelia couldn't stand her, for which she wouldn't blame her. But now all of a sudden this shy little flower was calling her up long distance. Why? Because she thought *Spencer* was about to leave her and she had heard through the parents that Lizzie and Roger had gone through some kind of similar trouble.

Well, goodness gracious, she had lots and lots of advice, Lizzie did! She sat in the living room, where Roger was reading the paper, going on and on about life and marriage and working things out—she must have been on the phone two hours, but she hoped she had helped. "God knows," she said to Cecelia, "I understand how it feels."

"Cecelia thinks Spencer's about to leave her," she informed Roger in a low voice.

Not as fast as I'll be leaving you, Roger thought grimly to himself.

He had to leave; he had planned to leave her that night, it would be all he could do to wait until her cousin Merry left. He was frozen with fear, freaked-out, crazed, tight, anxious, he was getting pains in his chest; he felt like an elephant was sitting on his chest. He didn't know what it meant. Every morning he would go down to the alleyway, get into his car, and burst out crying as he never had before, tears that seemed to well up from his toes, accompanied by loud moans and sobs. And yet he loved her! He just couldn't stand to be with her. He was terrified to be with her and he didn't know what he was terrified of. Leaving her wouldn't solve anything, but he couldn't be with her. All he knew was that he had a real problem and that he had to leave and he had to see a shrink. He had never reached rock bottom; he had always been the captain of every team, all his life. He had never done anyone any wrong. Now he seemed to be hurting everyone with everything he did. He was completely falling apart.

Her cousin Merry left early Sunday morning before they got up. Saturday she had helped Roger and Lizzie hang old family photographs in their room. "Why aren't you hanging up any pictures of Roger's family?" Merry had asked innocently, having no idea of the summer's events. In fact, she had kept saying all weekend how jealous she was of their life.

That morning Lizzie had touched his shoulder in bed and he had actually winced, then gotten up to go downstairs. She had lain in bed, throwing the water glasses that always accumulated on her side table at the wall. Of course they wouldn't break, they were gifts from Roger's mother and ugly and heavy and meant to be unbreakable. Finally on the second round she really whammed one and managed to break it into two large chunks.

When she went into the bathroom overlooking the alley, she saw him putting his toolbox into the back of the Peugeot. That's when she knew for sure. She went back into the bedroom and waited.

"I'm leaving," he said, coming into the room.

"I know," she said, sitting on the bed. She didn't feel like crying at all. She felt, she supposed, relief.

"Will you give me a divorce?" he asked, bursting into tears.

"Sure," she said, not sarcastically, but nicely. She

actually felt sorry for him. "Sure, I'll give you a divorce," and she took her sobbing husband into her arms.

"I'm so sorry, Lizzie, so sorry," he blubbered, "I don't want to hurt you. I'm so unhappy!" and so she comforted him, told him how he would feel better again someday, he had to believe that, the problem was he had never been down before. Go! Go! she kept thinking to herself. But instead she sent him out to buy a Sunday paper to take with him to where he was leaving her, the cabin in Maine.

Hope slept through the whole thing. Leslie, as always, was a wreck. She'd jumped between the two of them, turned white around her tightened mouth, and shook and shivered like something out of a Greek tragedy. Lizzie had eventually picked her up and was still carrying the trembling dog when she walked down Marlboro Street to meet Roger coming back from the store. At the sight of the two of them, Roger broke down again.

"Now, now," said Lizzie, and then to the whimpering dog, "Give your father a kiss."

Finally after the last good-byes and after she'd slipped her new wedding ring into his shirt pocket, he got into the Peugeot, and it wouldn't start.

"Can I borrow your car?" he asked through his tears.

Sure, she thought, why not, borrow my car to leave me, just go!

21

A Buck a Minute

The steering wheel was her face, and he kept stroking and stroking it, crying "Oh Lizzie! Oh Lizzie! Oh Lizzie!" over and over as he drove the bashed-up Subaru to Maine. Was this it? Was he nuts? Is this how all those crazy relatives of Lizzie's felt, right before they flipped out and got really happy because they were about to save the world? Is this how the zombies wandering around Brookhill had felt before the injections? No, he wasn't nuts—somehow he felt that the others probably wouldn't be searching inside the seat for exact change for the toll. Oh Lizzie! God, he wished she were really there to help him now—she would have some psychological theory about how *everybody* thinks his wife is a steering wheel, etc., etc. She, who said "I wish I were dead" when she forgot to bring a fork to eat supper with in front of the TV, would tell him not to worry, things always get better, just as she had that day, when, after all his promises, he was asking her for a divorce, begging her for a divorce, *she* was consoling *him*! But he couldn't be with her, don't ask him why, he had just known that he would explode if he didn't leave her, that he had to get a divorce or he would die. Now, of course, he wished he *were* dead! She had made him promise not to call her. *Promise* not to call. She had said she loved him but now she wanted to get over him—she didn't want to *know* him!

The night before, when he had sat in the Vendome Restaurant, across from the woman whose life he was about to ruin (and the cousin of the woman whose life he was about to ruin), an elephant sitting on his chest, as it had every second of the day for the last two weeks, he'd tried to cheer himself up by saying well, this is the bottom, at least it can't get any worse. But now, one day later, it was worse, so much worse! "No man is an island," his father had said. "You can't be out there alone with your feelings." Well, that's exactly where he was, out there in space with his feelings, except he didn't know what he felt except terror—terror of what, he couldn't say. He had never been at rock bottom, if indeed this was rock bottom, maybe it was going to get worse. It couldn't get worse, could it?

All he knew was that he had always been the leader, even when he had first come to PRV and no one was aware he was an athlete and they'd all gone out for the touch football game against Channel Five, someone had said, "Okay, Stoner's captain." He had always been the leader because he was decisive; he never wavered, never let a doubt or a technicality like a lack of knowledge get in the way of making a decision—no one really cared if you were right, it seemed, as long as you acted as though you believed you were, as long as you acted at all. This was all he asked for in life (or at least *now* it was all he asked for in life): to have the confidence to know what to do next.

But now he couldn't even decide whether to take Route 1 or Route 95 up to Maine. He had completely fallen apart. He was like those good-for-nothing guys Lizzie knew from Harvard who had no discernible occupation and spent the whole morning deciding where to have brunch and then (around the time the bill arrived) had a funny, pathetic story about losing their wallet on the subway.

He had to see a shrink, he was going to crawl on his stomach to the shrink; Lizzie would have been proud. And yet, he couldn't have stayed with Lizzie *and* seen a shrink; it didn't make sense, but it was true.

Somebody canceled, and he got in to see the shrink the very next day, Monday, after, of course, getting up at dawn to make the drive back from Maine to Boston. He'd gotten her name from his boss on "The Cafe." She was about sixty, with a thick European accent. She lived, where most shrinks apparently lived, in Cambridge. Her office was decorated in 1960s teak, and sure enough, just as Lizzie had described—the only reason he had noticed any of this was that Lizzie said all women shrinks of this era had the same office—in among the impressive books with embarrassing titles like *Female Sexuality* were lots of half-naked, carved figurines from her trips to Africa. Exactly like Rena's office (Rena was Lizzie's family shrink in *New York*, who you went to if you were screwed-up when you happened to be in New York; he hadn't dared ask where else they had family shrinks), except in the middle of Rena's, Lizzie said, had glared a copy of the album, *Hey, Hey, We're the Monkees!*, about which finally, after three years of therapy, Lizzie had broken down to ask, "Listen to the Monkees much?" Rena had children, of course; Lizzie said she had suspected as much from the variety of hair conditioners in the bathroom. You weren't supposed to ask shrinks questions about themselves according to Lizzie.

Roger's had thick black hair in a bun and wore long

silver earrings and some kind of black shiny cotton dress, quite stylish, nothing like the women her age in Greenwich, Connecticut, with their kelly green wraparound skirts and bright nylon headbands. Her name was Vrisslof—what did that make her, Russian? Possibly Jewish? Whatever she was, Dr. Vrisslof was perfect. She was a woman, but not a disapproving woman. He remembered what Lizzie had said about Rena, that she could make you feel good about murdering your mother, except, of course, in Rena's case, Rena'd *known* her mother.

One of the first things Vrisslof said to him, after they had the opening discussion about fee (which at sixty bucks a whack was quite a conversation-opener) was, after he had told her at great length how evil he was, "This is not a church, Meester Stoner." Oh yes, Vrisslof was the opposite of his mother, but old enough so, if you wanted to stretch it, she could have been his mother. Anyway, she was perfect. At sixty bucks a pop, why not.

Jesus, that was more than a buck a minute. He didn't have the money! How could he have the money when he'd spent the entire summer making that goddamn birdhouse? "Do not worry about the money," she had said, "you are not destitute; you will pay me later."

A buck a minute! He poured it all out, everything he could think to bring her up to date, straight for fifty minutes. All the awful things he'd done, Christ, she had to be made out of jelly to not disapprove! And yet, she wasn't disapproving, and it was great she wasn't disapproving because—he was the first to face it—he was a bad person! On and on he went; she couldn't get a nod in edgewise. He was running out of breath but afraid to stop lest she sneak a look at that old, grinding five-dollar-and-ninety-five-cent plastic clock from the Harvard Coop. Finally his time was up! She was rustling in her seat and reaching for her appointment calendar.

"So," he said panting, "what's the diagnosis, what's wrong with me? I mean, there it all is. What's the problem, what's the matter with me?"

"Why don't we make an appointment for next week," Dr. Vrisslof said, turning the pages of her calendar.

"But I don't feel any better!" he shouted. He didn't! He didn't feel any better!

"We will see each other . . . next Monday, at four?"

"But I don't think I can *make* it until then! I'm not going to last," he panicked. "I think I'm going to kill myself!"

"Oh, don't do that," she said. "It might hurt."

He spent the night at Bobby Metz's, a guy he'd known since his bartending days and couldn't have gotten along better with, in spite of the fact he had never said anything more profound to him than "Got any beer in the icebox?" It had been extremely embarrassing for him to explain his situation over the phone, but he hadn't known who else to call, and then when he'd arrived Bobby's parents were there, and after a couple of beers they'd asked Roger to drop them off on his way home. What could he do? He drove them home and then, on the way back to Bobby's, he stopped at a pay phone. It wasn't fair, he knew, but he just had to find out how Lizzie was doing. He was so worried about her. He dialed the number.

"Stoner Bar and Grill!" shouted some ass on the other end. Roger placed the receiver back on the hook. There had been quite a rollicking party going on in the background.

22

Mr. Beberch Discovers the Truth

Frankly, she could have lived the whole rest of her life in complete happiness without ever again setting eyes on Roger Stoner. Unfortunately, there was the little affair of Mr. Beberch and the $1,000 loan.

The saga of the $1,000 loan began on their wedding anniversary at the end of October, when, not feeling as bouncy as usual, she'd decided to buck herself up by asking for a raise. She was quite the accomplished professional these days, the pièce de résistance of her career being her television commercial for Jim Dandy Chicken, where in ten seconds she had had to inform the people in Springfield that even though Kentucky Fried Chicken had closed up shop, there was still a place around that sold fried chicken. Her first TV commercial! It had all been terribly exciting. On the down side, however, had been the fact that the entire budget was $500, not even enough to buy one lousy stock photo of a plate of chicken. "Generally, we just run the specials over this slide of the parking lot we have," the account executive

had informed her listlessly. But then Lizzie had come up
with the idea of dressing up Harry, who was six foot
seven, as a chicken and having him sit very seriously in
heavy glasses behind a desk reciting the special, as if he
were the guy from the H & R Block commercials pontifi-
cating about tax returns. All she had to get across was
that Jim Dandy sold chicken, and all Harry would have
to say was one line. Harry, who had played sax behind
Bonnie Raitt without a flicker of nervousness on the
Johnny Carson show; Harry, who had had all the leads in
the high school plays—how cruel, how brilliant, as
Prince Bounin in *Anastasia*, she still shivered to remember!—surely he could handle: "Jim Dandy here, why not
try our 'Chicken Pickin's' for $2.95. At these prices,
who's squawking?"

But of course, Harry was nothing if not intense, and
hours and hours they'd had to rehearse at the agency,
Harry reading the one line over and over (clutching desperately onto the "script" because he wasn't ready yet to
give up, as he put it, "the security of the written word"),
and the next morning she'd been awoken by a 6:00 A.M.
phone call, no hello, just Harry barking out fiercely at
the speed of light: "Jim-Dandy-here-why-not-try-our-
chicken-pickin's-for-two-ninety-five-at-these-prices-who's
squawking?" All *night* he'd been practicing, and later, at
the recording studio, he couldn't get the damn line right!
"Why not try our chicken squawkings—why not try our
slim pickin's—" Harry had bellowed in monotone, until
finally, finally, he'd gotten the words right, at which
point he'd cried out, "No, no! Let me do it again! I didn't
really *mean* it!"

Sales increased 40 percent at the Jim Dandy Restaurants—people had actually walked in to say it was the
worst commercial they had ever seen.

Her boss—who called her "Scarlett" because she

always looked like she was at a garden party sitting in
her office in a flowered dress, a couple of guys lounging
about her on the floor—was a twinkly man with white
hair who looked out his window every morning at the
giant New England Life Building facing him, with its
hundreds of row upon row of cell like windows, and
praised God he didn't have to work for a living. He
agreed she deserved a raise but said she'd have to take it
up with the new creative director, who'd been thrown
into the package when they'd merged with the big agency
from New York.

The new creative director told her that, while perhaps
she deserved a raise, he felt confident she would agree
that, at this point in time they all "had to band together
to see the merger through." Was she was supposed to
band together on $9,000 a year while this guy was seeing
the merger through on some six-figure New York salary?
There seemed to be plenty of money to be spent on those
new chirping phones she noticed, with 150 buttons
nobody understood, especially after the eager telephone
people trapped you into a one-hour lesson. "Well," she
said huffily, "I'm an independent woman now and I
might have to look elsewhere," and the creative director
had said, certainly, he would understand.

So she picked up the phone and called Smith, Reilly,
the rival agency that had almost hired her the year before
during a drunken lunch; everyone drank in advertising,
but at Smith, Reilly they had after-dinner drinks after
lunch. Much had been made at that jolly meal of the
coincidence of the fact that the creative director, Dermott
Shaunnessy, had gotten married on the exact same day as
Lizzie.

"Well," he said when she called, "made it to our second anniversary. Make it to yours?"

"Nope," she said gaily, adding in the same breath

that she was looking for a job, and Shaunnessy had said great, they were looking, too, how much money did she want?

She'd never *dreamed* there'd be a job available. Why would she ever leave A & F, which had been like a second home to her, which had stood by her those months when she was getting nothing done but dropping burning cigarettes onto her Diane Von Furstenberg dresses (thank God they were wraparounds)? She would be crazy to leave! So, cleverly, she asked for $18,000—double her salary. Great, Shaunnessy said, he'd get back to her after he took it up with Henry, the head of the agency.

That afternoon she was in with the new A & F creative director, jumping up and then lying down on the floor in her $200 suit, to illustrate this idea for a yogurt commercial she had, when her phone, in the next office, rang, or rather chirped. "Oh, I've got to go," she sang out, leaping up from the floor and dashing into her office, shutting the door tight. She somehow knew it would be Shaunnessy. "Hi," she said conspiratorily, whispering to be extra safe.

She was in the middle of her succinct, but detailed (names named, and, she realized later, bold lies stated about her current salary) conversation with Shaunnessy when the door to her office swung open to a stream of people shouting out their congratulations. It seemed that her phone had somehow gotten hooked into the fancy new PA system, and the entire conversation, in beautiful crystal clarity, had been broadcast into every office over three floors. At least it hadn't happened earlier during one of her intense, whispered conversations with Roger about whether he *had* or *hadn't* slept with Jean Stock. Even in her panic, she took a moment to be grateful for that.

Of course, she got the job; the problem was that now

she had to take it, even after the let's-stick-this-merger-out A & F creative director suddenly decided that she was "a breath of fresh air" and worth $20,000. But she felt honor-bound (incorrectly, but honor-bound nevertheless) to take the job at Smith, Reilly and, not without regret, gave her notice. But then an additional problem arose: Smith, Reilly couldn't hire her for six weeks. What was she to do for money?

It was then that she came up with the bright idea of getting herself a $1,000 loan to tide her over. After all, most of what she wrote about was how easy it was—how much *fun*, really—to call up your friendly bank and obtain a loan. Although she had been brought up by her carefully unmortgaged parents to believe any debt was bad, after a year in advertising she had learned that, evidently, nothing seemed to make people happier (fixing up their house with a jaunty tune, or leaving it all behind for that sun-drenched beach) than borrowing money from their smiling banker representative.

And then, as she was always bragging for the banks in her copy, you could get the entire transaction signed, sealed, and delivered, right over the telephone. She herself couldn't phone, of course, because she'd never really figured out her bank's name. It was written in some crazy script on the wall behind the tellers, but worse than that was the tricky way the bank managed to hide the date, so mainly what you did when you went in to make a withdrawal was ask around, "Anyone know the date?" It was the least accommodating bank in the world, but, in spite of all those ads about the warmth and friendliness of one bank as opposed to another, all that mattered in the end was proximity, and the bank was located on the ground floor of A & F's building, so everyone went there.

"So," Lizzie said, swinging into the armchair across the desk from a black-eyeglass-framed Mr. Beberch

(Where *did* people get these names? she wondered), and trying to affect a well-to-do-career-woman-cossetted-by-an-indulgent-husband kind of an air, "I just thought I'd like to establish a little credit for myself—I'm *always* using my husband's (a little humorous roll of the eye here for added veracity)—by taking out a little loan." Mr. Beberch asked if she had a job, and she said of course, and he'd beamed and said no problem, just fill out these forms and give "a look in" at the end of the week. She swished out, quite the grande dame.

When she gave "a look in" at the end of the week, she was dead drunk, coming back from her A & F good-bye lunch. She teetered in with what she could only pray looked like a swagger of confidence, and after a danger-ous swerve or two, made it with a sigh of relief to Mr. Beberch's guest swivel chair. Her disheveled reflection in the plate glass behind him was not encouraging, but worse was the look on Mr. Beberch's face.

"But won-wonna gimme da money?!!" she cried out when she received the devastating news. Well, Mr. Beberch said, she hadn't told him she was changing jobs now, had she? at which point she burst out into uncontrollable sobs.

"I lied! I lied!" she cried wrenchingly, "But it sholdna matter, I making two times my sal'ry!" and then, she was sorry to say, she turned a bit nasty, making remarks about all those twenty-four-hour-no-nonsense-as-easy-as-one-two-three loans she was always writing about, where were they when she needed them, she wanted to know! Mr. Beberch remained unmoved. Finally she dissolved again into pitiful tears.

"Wha am I gonna do!" she blubbered, and Mr. Beberch, softening at last, suggested quietly that she might get that nice husband of hers to co-sign the loan, and tearfully, she nodded her assent.

"Everything is *great*!" she told Roger over the phone,

"great!" She was relieved to hear things were not great with him, just as she'd been relieved when she'd read Roger's desperate little missive the month before. *Pret-ty suicidal,* she'd sung to herself, before tossing the letter out. It wasn't that she wished him ill, exactly; she just couldn't help being a bit buoyed by the knowledge that he wasn't out there having a really great time. She knew this was callous, but callous had been the wave of the future for her, ever since she'd watched the Subaru pull out of the alleyway, and rushed upstairs, Leslie gripping her shoulder like a cat, to call Roger's father for the last time.

No, Roger said over the phone, he was still miserable, worse than ever, didn't know what he was going to do, wished he were dead. Oh, the tiny shot of joy that burst from her heart as she'd pressed for the gory details! Dear God, she was a bad person, but there it was, she was happy, and he was unhappy, just as the magazines had promised, the one who leaves *is* the one who suffers in the end. Well, she'd been waiting and waiting for that end part, and now here it was at last.

The big thing, she carefully instructed Roger over the phone, was not to let on they were no longer married— she simply could not stress this enough. She couldn't afford to be caught in yet another web of lies with Mr. Beberch.

When she met up with Roger and Mr. Beberch at the bank the next morning, she had absolutely no reaction to the fact that here was the man she had married and lost; she was too busy making the effort to appear casually conjugal in front of Mr. Beberch, as if she had just shared a homey cup of coffee with Roger minutes before. Mr. Beberch beamed at them as he handed Roger the papers to sign. She beamed back, then turned to address Roger in the most offhand yet in-on-each-other's-innermost-secrets-like manner, so as not to let on she had not laid eyes upon her "spouse" in two months.

"So," Lizzie said intimately, if a bit loudly, to Roger, "seen any good movies lately?"

The next day Roger saw Vrisslof.

"Maybe I should try getting back with Lizzie," he said.

"You must be out of your mind!" Vrisslof said.

"*That's* what I've been trying to tell you."

23

The Pipes Burst

Tuesday nights they did five shows, back to back, three minutes apart. Between shows Roger would hear, "One minute to air!" and his heart would be thumping and he would be thinking how he had completely and utterly fallen apart, and then he would hear, "Thirty seconds!" and then "Fifteen seconds!" and he would scream inside "I wish I were *dead*!" and then, "Ten seconds!" and the stage manager would start flashing fingers to countdown, as the live music rolled and the cameras, three of them, were being cut right and left, finally settling upon Roger, who would cry out ecstatically: "Hi! How are you? Welcome to The Cafe! I'm Roger Stoner, and we're going to have a *great* show tonight!"—and he would be off and running, adrenaline going like crazy, no more thinking, until the end of the fifth show, when he would say to the bartender, "Pour me a beer," and keep drinking, until the crowd had gone home and the lights were turned off, and down he would go to the men's room to wash off his pancake makeup.

Then he'd weave home in the Peugeot to his hovel in

Watertown, the room he rented from a nice old Italian couple in their single-family house. He'd stumble down the cement walkway along the side of the clapboard house to the back door and up the stairs to the second floor, where he walked through a bathroom into the room where he resided with a refrigerator, the institutional desk he had had as a child, and the pea green corduroy couch, the one piece of furniture he had taken from the town house. Lizzie had said in the note she'd pinned to the couch that he was *more* than welcome to the pea green (the mainstay of his decor back then, even down to the stripe in his sheets—he supposed he'd been trying for a masculine color) geometric shag rug he and his mother had picked out in his bachelor days, but for some reason, even though he knew it would have made Lizzie's day, he hadn't been able to take it. God, it was lonely in that dreary room! He would cry so hard at night that he would have to bury his head in his pillow because he was living in someone else's house. His bedroom was right next to the landlords', their bathroom pipe ran down his wall, he could hear their step, the low mumble of their voices—he was aware, it seemed, of their every movement, yet he almost never saw them, slinking in and out of the house as he did late at night and early in the morning, leaving his rent check, almost furtively, in the mailbox every month.

On the weekends, without work to occupy him, he probably would have jumped off a cliff, if the pipes hadn't burst in the Maine cabin. Generally there weren't any projects to do in Maine in the winter, except for shoveling the snow off the roof—one time he had fallen, like a cartoon character, head first off the roof past a window, as Lizzie and guests had looked on with horror. But now with the pipes freezing and exploding all over the cabin, well, here was something to get his hands on.

"Have to get up to Maine to work on the pipes," he could always tell Jean Stock in case she should get any ideas about wanting to spend some time with him. Generally, he dropped by her apartment a couple of nights a week, but he didn't like to think of them as technically "going out," not that he would have dared voice this to Jean, who was constantly pouring forth with gripes about their "relationship." "So when are you getting divorced?" she'd once dared to ask, but that time, at least, one look from him had shut her up.

For, on the one hand, as time passed he still seemed to bear no ill will toward Lizzie—he couldn't find it in his heart to blame her for anything—on the other hand, he was disliking Jean Stock more and more as the days went by. He knew she was messed up by the fact that her twin sister had drowned when they were little, run across a street into a river while their mother was on the phone (and then, of course, the father had never forgiven the mother)—he was sorry, truly sorry—but did it give someone the right to be so disagreeable for the rest of her life? She would yell at him all the time, crazy things, like accusing him of having an affair with the executive producer of "The Cafe," a sixty-year-old woman! "I don't get it," he would say to her, "I say A and you say Z. I don't see how anything you say has anything to do with anything I say." Sometimes to appease her, "to spend more time with her," he would take her out to Tony's for a beer and something to eat, before going back to her apartment and sleeping with her. Sitting in the booth at the small family restaurant in Brighton, she would rage at him vitriolically about how nobody *cared* in the way that she and her friend Suzanne, a tape editor, did! How only *they* (Suzanne and she) had any concern for the disadvantaged kids in the world; only *they* were willing to put in extra time working on news stories about handicapped kids. On and on and on she would go—he would put up with it, figuring he was a bad person and deserving of whatever abuse came his way, but finally he would say, "All right, all right, I get your point!" in a rather unencouraging way. Once she had screamed—right in the middle of a family restaurant—"Do you think I'm a lesbian?" A *lesbian*? He thought they'd been discussing poor kids!

The truth was, long hair and cowboy boots notwithstanding, Jean Stock had no style. He supposed she couldn't help it; her family had made their money in linoleum. Jesus, he *was* a snob! After all those years of wearing Ban-Lon body shirts and living in working-class neighborhoods and going out with girls he could never bring home, when it came down to it, he was a snob. For all her going to Bennington College and smoking pot and wearing jeans with leotard tops she managed to be tacky *and* pretentious at the same time. She might be a hippie, but that didn't mean she wasn't an asshole.

So he thanked God in heaven when the pipes burst in Maine and up he could drive on a Friday night, to get up early on Saturday morning and work straight through the day and well into the night. What was gratifying was that it was particularly frustrating work because, as he learned much later, he was using the wrong solder: First he would drain all the pipes, then solder all the joints, turn on the pipes, and there would be three or four leaks, water shooting out leaving both the house and Roger soaking wet. Then he'd start all over again on a job that, with the right solder, should have taken up no more than a single long weekend, but with the wrong soder he was able to stretch out over an entire winter of weekends. Plus, with the wrong solder, you really had to concentrate on what you were doing—it was like live television, with no room for thinking over and over, I'm a total wreck, I want to kill myself—the chant that went round and round his head on a normal day.

It was all he could think about, that he was a wreck, not why nor how, just the fact itself. Even his shrink had told him he sounded like a broken record. Were shrinks allowed to express such opinions? He remembered Lizzie's saying that Rena was always trying to boost her self-esteem with encouraging remarks like, "Lizzie darling, you're neurotic, but neurotic is good!" whereas all he ever got was shouted down.

Another time he'd gone bursting into Vrisslof's office saying, "You must think I'm an awful person, wreaking havoc on everyone's life!" The shrink had looked at him sternly. "What do you think I am, a *priest*? I am *not* a priest!" she had said. He was still nonplussed by the idea that he could discuss things without being judged for them. Most of the time, though, she wouldn't say anything. "Do you think I'm crazy?" he'd ask her. "What do *you* think?" she would retort.

But up at the cabin those winter weekends, he found respite. He got so immersed in the pipes that he wouldn't break until about ten at night, when he would suddenly realize he was ravenous and drive himself over to the Appleseed Inn, the joint off Route 1, order dinner at the bar, and eat and drink one scotch after another while watching TV and chatting to Patrick the bartender, or Nancy the waitress, who would always ask, as Roger was downing his one hundredth straight scotch, "So where's Elizabeth?"

"Up at the cabin," Roger would slur back, until finally the fourth weekend in a row that she'd asked, he said, "Actually we're separated."

"And you have been ever since you've been coming here Saturday nights, haven't you?" Nancy had said, though luckily she hadn't pursued the point. But mainly

Roger exchanged drunken pleasantries with Patrick: "So, big snowstorm last week," or, "Got to get my chainsaw fixed"—the kind of chitchat he would have with Guy the tree chopper, with long pauses between, that always made Roger feel he was at one with these people of the country, really just the same in his baseball cap and his simple unambitious life. He liked to think of himself as coming up to Maine and simply blending in. Of course, he supposed he couldn't exactly blend in anymore now that he'd put Millwood, Maine, on television, now that everyone knew he was a producer from Boston, the cat having come out of the bag when he'd decided to do a segment on the Fourth of July up in Millwood two summers back. He remembered how Stu, who ran the variety store in town, or rather who was married to the woman who ran the store, had been all over the place in his Hawaiian shirt when Roger had arrived with the camera crew. Stu, who always called out, "Hey, slapshot!" when he saw Roger coming down the aisle. The next week Roger had had to break it to Stu that he'd ended up on the cutting-room floor. "Aw, that's all right," Stu had said, "I was on in some places. Some people I know in Worcester, they saw me on TV."

Well, Roger had lost his anonymity with putting the whole town on television, but it had been a great piece, quite poignant. He could be quite poignant in fact when it came to putting other people's lives on TV, quite upstanding too. One reviewer had called his documentaries, ". . . moving and intensely moral. Stoner has high standards and holds the world to them." Ha! He remembered once smoking a joint while he and Lizzie had been watching his film on the drug dealer and Roger's voice-over coming on, "So where do you draw the line with drugs?" and Lizzie giving him a sidelong glance.

He thought of his documentary on Vietnam vets—it

still made him want to cry to think about it. When it came down to it, he supposed, all he hoped to accomplish in life was to get people to cry when they watched his shows—well, might as well be honest: He also craved the recognition of his peers. After he'd quit the insurance job and didn't know what to do, his godfather, who he realized later was an alcoholic, had told him to sit down and write a list of the things he had wanted in life. At the top of his list, to his surprise, Roger had put "prestige." He had thought his godfather was a pretty cool guy after that, and then the following year the godfather had shot himself. Not that anyone had particularly remembered to tell Roger about it; if he hadn't happened to see it the next day in the paper, he wouldn't have known.

If he cared so much about what people thought of him, why, then, was he doing "The Cafe" and making a goddamn fool of himself every goddamn night of the week? Why was he learning how to "address" the vegetables in a wok, or interviewing some so-called time-management expert from a deodorant company? Well, nothing he did made any sense anymore. The shrink said he needed approval because he'd never gotten the approval of his mother. "You must be very angry with women," she had said.

"Of course not!" Roger had protested, but then seeing her point, hadn't stopped to pause for a breath until the session was over.

At any rate, the point was, he, Mr. Blend-in, had put Millwood on TV and now he couldn't go into the hardware store without someone coming up to him with a great idea for a new show. Still he liked to think when he sat at the bar with Patrick, Patrick felt he was just another guy like him—though, of course, Roger had to admit, if he had Patrick's life he'd probably shoot himself in the head, not that he might not be shooting himself in the head anyway. Whittling that birdhouse all that past summer had kind of convinced him that, truth be known, Roger didn't really fit in as a Maine type. Not, of course, that he even knew what the Maine type was, particularly after he learned one night from Nancy about all the wife-swapping in town. "Just because they live in Maine doesn't mean they're all wholesome," Lizzie had said once.

Things were generally pretty peaceful at the Apple-seed, although one time that winter there'd been a young guy sitting at the bar who couldn't get his first sip down before getting on Roger's case. "I live in a trailer," he had announced defensively looking straight at Roger, who'd had the intelligent expression on his face he always got when he was about ten scotches to the wind; it was another trait of Roger's that the only time he ever looked profound was when he was nearly brain dead with alcohol.

"Oh, that's great," Roger had said absently.

"Yeah, well, I know *some* people like to look down on other people who happen to live in a trailer," the kid retorted.

"Not me!" said Roger with sudden enthusiasm, thinking, All I want is for you to shut the hell up so I can finish getting drunk in peace, but adding aloud, perhaps a bit de troply, "No I think living in a trailer would be great!"

"Oh yeah, what are you, some kind of wise guy?!" The kid had jumped up with from his seat, getting more and more worked up. Christ, Roger would have left then and there, if he hadn't had to contemplate getting off the barstool. The hardest part of his Saturday nights was getting off that barstool. There was a whole different equilibrium to sitting down and standing up, he had realized one night; it was funny how you never heard people discussing it, but Roger, Roger had pondered it on many a drunken Saturday night, once venturing off the usual simple conversational terrain to share it with Patrick, who had nodded sagely in the way that led Roger to believe that what he'd said was probably a bit more along the line of "eerrrpout bout brrrst?" But finally it would be two in the morning and he would have no choice and then he would, oh so carefully, lift himself off the stool, his heart lurching as it did a little good-bye swivel, and gently place first one foot then another on Mother Earth.

But that night Roger didn't have to worry about getting off the barstool, because the next time he looked up from his drink, it was into the fist of the kid with the trailer, and then he was knocked cold.

"How are you?" asked Dr. Vrisslof that Monday as Roger sat down.

"Fine!"

"Fine? You're not fine or you wouldn't be here."

"Jesus, I was brought up to be polite! I'm not going to answer people with a whole rash of shit, I'm not going to sit there and unload on someone who asks me how I am."

"You don't express yourself toward anyone," said Vrisslof in an exasperated tone. "You don't have a relationship with anyone. For example, I have no idea about what you feel about me."

"You?" said Roger. "What do I think of *you*?" What was he supposed to say, she was his shrink, he didn't have any feelings toward *his shrink*! Jesus, nobody understood. It just wasn't *natural* for him to have feelings; he marveled at people who could have feelings, let alone express them. He would have liked to stick up just once for the side of suppressing your feelings. Sure, it might not be a particularly useful one in the long run, but in the short run—and he personally set great store by the short run—doing something active like fixing the pipes in Maine as a way of forgetting your feelings not only helped you feel better, but let you accomplish something to boot. Ever since he hadn't been able to suppress his feelings, he'd felt like hell and gotten nothing done.

Now here he was like a goddamn three-year-old trying to learn how to express himself. There was Vrisslof just waiting, determined to get an answer. Well, first he had to dredge up some feelings. He had to think before he could tell what he was feeling, he was trying to think hard now about it. Of course there was the general feeling that his insides were in a vise that someone kept turning and turning—that was the basic backdrop of his emotions these days. Did that count as a feeling, he wondered, could he possibly get off the hook with that one? He sneaked a look at Dr. Vrisslof. Probably not. Still, if you were going through that, how were you supposed to have time to have "feelings" about your shrink? How did he *feel* about Dr. Vrisslof? He searched his brain as best he could. Nothing, he couldn't find anything, not a single solitary thing.

"I like you?" he tried hopefully.

24

Charlotte Has a Theory

Her new roommate was a girl named Lulu, who appeared to live exclusively on three-pack chocolate chip cookies and white wine. She was an assistant art director at A & F and very good, in spite of a lazy streak that caused her, after working long and hard on a project, at its finish to just slap the picture on the posterboard any which way. She'd actually been told by the head art director that she hadn't been promoted because she dressed so sloppily. "Why don't you dress, like, well, like Elizabeth?" he had suggested. Lizzie *had* certainly dolled herself up, kindness of Roger's Saks charge, but Lulu, who often arrived at work in dripping wet hair because she couldn't be bothered to dry it, hadn't held it against her. That was the miracle of Lulu—she was utterly without malice and, at the same time, couldn't have been more screwed-up—exactly perfect, in Lizzie's eyes! She'd liked Lulu the moment she'd first set eyes upon her hyperventilating in the ladies' room.

For some reason the moving in of Lulu, which transpired in December, produced in Lizzie a sudden air of industry, with the result that she came up with a bevy of housekeeping plans to keep the town house looking nice. All Lulu needed to give her, Lizzie figured, was just one hour a week to help her clean. Dutifully, mournfully, Lulu had followed her about one Saturday as Lizzie showed her how you sprayed the Pledge, then dusted, eliciting only the faintest grunts of response, until she got to the part on how you sponged out the toilet bowl. "Ewww!" Lulu had screamed, "you put your *hand* down the toilet?"

Lulu and she agreed it would be "cringy" at their age if they were like college roommates, having dinner together every night, so they went their separate ways, Lulu disappearing in the evening, semi-ironed in jeans and man's sports jacket to "The Room," a bar in Harvard Square with woodshavings on the floor, where the hip and the derelict mingled, raggedly indiscernible from one another. Lizzie had been dragged there once, and had sat sternly facing a wall while an enormous man, a kerchief tied over his balding head like the wolf in Red Riding Hood, had wooed her, cupping his hands in an "o" while graphically describing the birth of his child. If she wasn't tempted to join Lulu and her friends, Lizzie was very glad to have Lulu living in the room next to hers—"the apartment," they called it—with the two denim couches Lulu had found on the street one day, the TV, and, of course, the inevitable impossible-to-rig-up stereo system required even of the tone-deaf in the 1970s, with speakers large enough for a dance hall.

Yes, she was very thankful to have Lulu there, it was so *relaxing*. It meant she could take a little break from bringing guys home from work and making them fires in the fireplaces—of which she had four, all to herself. Unfortunately, while Roger had provided her with plenty of firewood with which to entertain her suitors, he had neglected to provide her with any kindling, with the result that her fires would roar magnificently on crumpled newspaper for two full minutes, then peter out to nothing. But it didn't matter, she supposed, just as it didn't matter how many drinks she had, for after a few grapples on the living-room floor, the stereo blaring and Hope jumping on top of each candidate, she'd sent them all home.

Not that she had any morals—she thought nothing of inviting every married man known to God to the parties she was always throwing at the spur of the moment. Even the caring Chas from PRV had been summoned forth, the star guest for the party celebrating Roger's final departure, although he'd seemed a bit dour in his lumber jacket and long face, next to the spiffy high spirits from A & F. And yet she'd been so perfectly willing to overlook anything that night from Chas—his wife, his girlfriend(s), his self-seriousness, even his lack of any real interest in her—anything but his commiseration. But commiseration was what she got, when turning to him in glowing triumph, having miraculously, with a pair of tongs, transferred a burning log from the living-room fireplace to the dining-room fireplace, he'd dashed her merriment with a deep-toned, "How are *you*, Elizabeth?"

What Nick and his roommate, Les, in the apartment upstairs made of all her goings on, she didn't dare ask. She did suspect "in the privacy of her own home" would not have been a key phrase in their opinion on the matter, as there was only one common staircase in the house, and her living-room doors, which elegantly slid together from either side, had a tendency to elegantly slide apart of their own accord whenever activity before the fire increased. Nick was their tenant from the Watertown house, who when he'd heard what they were charging for the Back Bay apartment had said he'd *never* pay that kind of rent, but two weeks later had sheepishly moved in. She'd been developing quite a little crush upon Nick until he'd invited her to his big party the week after she and Roger had split up, and she'd arrived all duded up to face one hundred guys crammed into the apartment looking at her blankly. She liked Nick and Les, although she couldn't say the same for Les's father, a red-faced businessman who visited from time to time, crawling up the staircase at 2:00 A.M. slobbering drunk, once lunging into her bedroom, which was situated at the bottom of the stairs to the third-floor apartment of Les and Nick, with the boozy hope of crawling into bed beside her.

Of course, everyone thought she was fair game these days. How could she blame them, the way she was dressing and acting? No wonder one of her bosses had put his hand up her slitted skirt casually one night when they were out drinking, and the other had told her to play an "away game" when she was complaining of the bitterness at home between Lulu and her because their agencies were pitching the same account. An away game? She hadn't even known what he meant; all she'd been able to think of was her father listening to a White Sox game on his transistor radio.

And yet, even without a boyfriend, she had been surprisingly happy since Roger had left. It was the first time that something other than a guy had been important in her life; she began to see how people in the world were able to get up in the morning and go on living when they weren't in love. What a novel idea to care about something other than boys! Sometimes as she bustled about at work, her mind percolating with arresting phrases about NOW accounts, she felt rather like a heroine from one of the old movies, strong (and sleek-waisted) against the world.

She began, in a strength bordering on hubris, to feel

magnanimous even toward Roger. She had blossomed, after all, while he had gotten stuck further in the mud— the least she could do was let him know how happy she was. He would be glad to know she was happy; if nothing else, that would make him feel better. And then, niggling in her brain was the thought: What was the point of being over Roger if he didn't know it? For months she hadn't spoken to him, hadn't so much as turned on the TV—he was on *every* night—to watch him learning disco steps in his bell-bottom trousers. She hadn't dared, because she'd known it would set her back. Now, at last, everything had changed.

But when she called Roger up in Maine spur of the moment at 4:00 A.M. on New Year's Eve, waking him out of a sound sleep (he'd actually been *dreaming* he was asleep) to tell him she was over him, instead what came out of her mouth was: Would he stand by her if she ever had cancer! She was drunk, of course, back from a party, and she was crazy, but, fortunately, Roger was crazy too. He had joined right in; they had both cried on the phone for two hours. She was so young! they had sobbed, forgetting, of course, that she had never actually had cancer in any form. Finally, as they were drying their tears, she'd mentioned she'd heard about this couple who had broken up for a year and a half and then gotten back together and had two kids. "They did? They did?" Roger had wept in joy.

But this depressed her more than anything. It all depressed her, all the nice things Roger had said, because she knew they had nothing whatsoever to do with anything. It was just round and round the mulberry bush again. She remembered protesting to Carsy at the beginning, back when Roger was living at the Ma and Pa Motel and taking her out every other night, "But Roger keeps telling me he loves me!" and Carsy had said,

"Look at his actions, not at what he says." Roger had said he loved her, but he'd walked out. He'd said he loved her, but it hadn't kept him from sleeping with Jean Stock. Carsy had been right, and after Roger had left for good she had never gone back to see Carsy again.

But why should any of it bother her if she were over Roger? Clearly she was not over Roger, maybe would never be. In any event, this was the end of her ever thinking she could call up Roger for a friendly chat—hadn't she always said they could never just be friends? She hung up the phone, feeling a terrible sadness. The next day she called Dr. Trumbull. She wanted a divorce.

She didn't feel particularly strong or sleek-waisted when her birthday rolled around on March 31, generally the worst day in the year, anyway you looked at it, but particularly when you were twenty-eight and about to become a divorcée. Nevertheless, she perked up a little when news reached her at work that flowers had been sent to her; they were waiting for her at the desk. An unknown admirer? Roger? She rushed down the stairs; she was a firm believer in the dark before the dawn. Perhaps this was a turning point, a break in a certain dull, depressive spirit that, she hated to admit, had settled upon her after New Year's. Surely something good was about to happen—if not very good, at least a little good. Even if the flowers were from Roger—she preferred them not to be from Roger, because if so, they would only be a pathetic peace offering—still it would be better than nothing.

It was a *corsage,* for Christ's sake, and it was from her parents. Her parents! The nicest people in the world, but total morons. What was she supposed to do, go around wearing a corsage all day as if she was off to the senior prom? Her parents! Masters of the oblivious eye, still living in blissful ignorance of her day-to-day life. She was supposed to put on a corsage now and flaunt it around the ad agency? "Oh, who's *that* from?" people would ask. "My parents," she was supposed to say with bashful pride? Oh God, it was all so sad, her parents trying so hard and as usual doing exactly the wrong thing. The corsage never had a chance; she threw it away while she was still in motion walking down the hall to her office. The phone was ringing. She couldn't stop her heart leaping a little, again with hope. Hadn't she learned anything? Who else—it was her parents, singing "Happy Birthday" over the phone.

The problem with Dr. Trumbull was that he, like her parents ("If only you would get that hair off your forehead so we could see your pretty face!"), was just a little too interested in when she was going to get a haircut. "Well," he said one Saturday morning after she had finally made it to the hairdresser's, "don't *you* look nice!" and then he'd proceeded to allude encouragingly to her tidier look three times during the session. Sometimes, too, she wanted to tell him he wasn't fooling anyone when he looked right at her, his nostrils flaring and his eyes tearing, so proud of himself for swallowing that yawn. But he was cute, the way all fathers of her acquaintance invariably were. She particularly got a kick of that full-length fur coat he wore—a WASP man in a fur coat! "I like your coat, Dr. Trumbull," she finally could not resist saying one day, and he'd mumbled embarrassedly something about a trip to Russia.

It was quite probable that she and Dr. Trumbull would not be making psychotherapeutic history, and yet, she felt safe with him—he wasn't going to start things off by boring into her about sexual details, like that Dr. Carsy. Very likely it would not be necessary to tell Dr.

Trumbull about how she'd slept with Miller Cross once by accident on the living-room floor. Dr. Trumbull wasn't even particularly interested in discussing the divorce—of course, this was something of a problem in that the whole *reason* she was going to a shrink was to discuss the divorce. "Please give me the courage to get a divorce!" she'd cried out during her first visit. "Won't change your feelings," Dr. Trumbull had said dismissively.

Oh, yes, her feelings, her feelings were a great help now, weren't they? It was so gratifying that she'd figured out that she still loved Roger (loved him *more* than when she'd married him), and worse, he still loved her, in his crippled little way, but the point was: *it didn't make any difference.* They were never going to be together. Finally, finally she had gotten this enigmatic but intractable fact into her poor little pea brain. And yet, nothing in her romantic fantasies had prepared her for this. How could two people love each other and not be able to be together? Two people who weren't only *not* married to other people, but who were still married to each other! If only they'd had World War II to come between them, so they could love each other and be apart nobly! But, tragically, there was nothing preventing their union, nothing except the minor but irrefutable fact that Roger couldn't *stand* to be with her.

How was she to reconcile herself to this? Where was the fairy tale with such an ending, where was the Jane Austen novel? She instructed herself to remember good old Tommy McGuire who, in their day, had come to see her only once a week at midnight—but oh, those intense looks across the Adams House dining hall that kept her going the rest of the week! "I believe in manifest destiny," he had said in one of the rare moments they were actually together, and she, too, had known in her heart that one day she and Tommy would be together forever, and then, three months after they'd graduated, he'd gotten engaged to his high school girlfriend! All the great guys she'd turned down waiting for Tommy McGuire, two years of Harvard down the drain. No, if she fooled herself into waiting for Roger to find himself at last, the next thing you knew, he'd come running in, his face boyishly aglow to announce that he'd met this great girl and he was in love, truly in love, and could finally allow himself to be close to someone!

None of this did she share with Dr. Trumbull, who to her great relief didn't seem particularly interested in Roger. "Nothing we can do about him," he said. So instead she spent most of her Saturdays trying to get to Brookhill from Back Bay via public transportation (the Subaru with its dead battery out to pasture in her alleyway under a blanket of black snow) to discuss what *she* wanted in life. She said she wanted to be a writer, although she had not written a single word since the glorious four-week stint in college (right before she'd met the trumpet player). Dr. Trumbull said this was just fine, but she could tell he was thinking that a nice girl like her (and with such a nice haircut!) ought to get married and have children—he actually said she would find herself feeling more secure in life after she'd married and had kids. Of course, this was what she herself had so unfashionably believed since infancy. The problem was, she reminded him, she *had* married, and it hadn't worked! So now, it was better to want to be a writer. Okay, said Dr. Trumbull, she could be Erma Bombeck, behind whose words always lurked the comforting churn of a washing machine.

With great drama, she announced to her parents that she was "proceeding with the divorce proceedings."

Somewhat to her surprise, they were very understanding, particularly her father, who you could tell (in spite of his wife's admonishing "Ben!"s) was still absolutely furious at his son-in-law for leaving his daughter. All her life, to her hair-pulling frustration, her parents had carefully tried "to see the other person's point of view," but now finally, she heard not a peep in defense of Roger. Even her parents had given up, their fervor spent in the letter-writings of the summer before, nearly a year ago, when hope still sprung eternal enough for her mother to write Roger that she loved him no matter what had happened and always would. Back had come the letter from Roger to "Charlotte and Ben" (Roger's walking out that April seemed to have catapulted him onto a first-name basis with her parents) explaining that none of the break up was their daughter's fault. This letter, glowing with their daughter's praises, had against it the unfortunate fact that in the interim between her parents' letter and Roger's, Roger had left their daughter for good. Even her mother (who would "always love Roger, no matter what") had not found it in her to write Roger back.

No, on the subject of Roger there had been a respectful silence for months, and the news of her decision to divorce did not elicit even a whimper of protest. And yet when she arrived at her parents' for Easter, she found all her wedding pictures, which had been discreetly put away after the break up, were now beaming at her from the piano, the bookshelves, even cozying up to the baby pictures on her mother's bureau—although she was pleased to notice that her father had refrained from hanging the enormous, expensively framed baseball picture Roger had inexplicably given him for Christmas, the only present Roger gave anyone in the family that year.

What was she to say? She knew this display was based on some new theory of her mother's. Her mother

was always coming up with theories about her children—
Spencer and Cecelia's marriage problems had vanished,
went a recent theory, once they'd started sitting down to
a home-cooked dinner every night—for her children were
still her life, even though they were supposedly grown-
up. Her mother had probably kept her father up one
night earnestly discussing how best to deal with Lizzie's
divorce, and this, this is what they'd come up with? But
what was it supposed to *mean*? Apparently, nobody was
about to let her in on the secret. Not a word was mentioned about the divorce or the pictures all weekend,
until finally, as Lizzie was being driven to the train station, she mentioned, for the record, that she had happened to notice that the wedding pictures were suddenly
out again. Her mother paused a second, and then out it
came, what she'd finally landed on to explain how anyone could divorce her lovely daughter.

"Roger's just not well," said her mother.

25

What Happens in the End

She woke up to the gay thought that it was April 20,
exactly one year since her husband had walked out, and
where had she gotten? Absolutely nowhere. Well, not
nowhere—after all, Roger was having mahogany cabinets built for her in the kitchen to the tune of $8,000.

"But I don't *want* the mahogany cabinets!" she had
said to Dr. Trumbull.

"Take them," Dr. Trumbull had said. "It's all he can
give you right now."

It drove her absolutely crazy. Why was he fixing up
the goddamn kitchen, and since when did anyone need
mahogany kitchen cabinets? She didn't even like them—
there was something tacky about new mahogany in her
mind, especially in a kitchen. Not to mention the fact
that she didn't even have an *oven*, just the toaster ovens
Roger had bought her that sent out competing aromas of
the various Shake 'n Bake flavors whenever she turned
them on. But the worst part was, every night when she

came home from work, she had to ooh and aah over the craftsmanship for the sensitive young cabinetmaker— some hippie-type Roger had dug up who called himself an "artisan" and tiptoed about tapping and nudging around the sandpaper oh-so-delicately until *eight o'clock at night.* This meant when she came *back* from her jog she had to ooh and aah yet again. Easy for Roger to work off his guilt by giving her the damn cabinets, why didn't he pitch in on some of the oohing?

She was jogging now *twice* a day, four miles in the morning, four miles at night. Hope and Leslie thought they'd died and gone to heaven. She'd come home from work and think, "If I have to jog tonight I'm going to kill myself, but if I *don't* jog tonight I'm going to kill myself," and up the stairs she would go to don her jogging rags. Jesus, she'd actually stood around comparing training schedules the other day with Bill Rodgers, the marathon runner, who was doing some spots with Smith, Reilly. Lizzie, who had never gotten further in swimming than advanced beginners; Lizzie, who had only passed gym in high school because she had clean socks. Even Lulu said she was getting to feel guilty that *she* didn't jog four miles twice a day, too. But the jogging had been her only hope. She didn't really grasp the business about endorphins, but she did know that when she came back from her jog at night and put her "Barbecue-Style" chicken breast into the toaster oven, her personal life might have been exactly as terrible as it had been before she'd jogged, but frankly, she no longer cared. Forget all her psychological theories: No wonder Roger had missed the grapplings of adolescence in his teens—he'd been a jock.

One year since Roger had left her. She loved her work; she was a great success. She no longer felt the desperate need to party. So why wasn't she feeling any better? Unless she was working, or had just jogged, she in fact felt worse. Well, that wasn't true, she supposed, at least she didn't feel anxious anymore; anxiety after all rested on a certain amount of hope. That was what she felt, hopeless, and deadened, and yet perfectly able to function. No, she hadn't fallen apart, the worst thing that could happen to her had happened and she'd reacted, well, normally, getting up in the morning and going about her business, instead of staying in bed day after day eating ice cream sandwiches, as she had in college, waiting for the magic moment when she would go crazy and be carried off to the sanitorium like Natalie Wood in *Splendor in the Grass,* to emerge beautiful in a big white hat, engaged to her psychiatrist. It seemed she would *not* be joining the clan at Brookhill or Cousin Maddie in upstate New York, chanting with the Buddhist monks. After all the shrinks (her father used to moan about all the money he's spent for three of his children to find out they were not manic-depressive, when he could have told them as much for free), it turned out in the end that she was a normal person. Even Dr. Trumbull had told her she was a garden-variety neurotic, but instead of its being a relief, she was embarrassed to say, it had been a disappointment. It appeared she was just going to have to go on with life like everybody else.

It didn't seem to matter, either, that, as regarded her decision to divorce, she was clearly in the right. No one, not even Roger, had argued with her on that. A divorce would give her the strength to get on with her life, she'd thought. So where was her spirit? Her reason to live? My God, she actually wasn't interested in guys. Even when Miller Cross suddenly sent her twelve long-stem roses, she didn't care. Even when Tom Koch—whom she had wanted to *marry* before going out with Roger, whom she had thrown herself at during the marriage—even when

Tom Koch arrived out of the blue one day with the news that his therapist thought that he actually *had* had an affair with Lizzie (Where had she been? she thought to herself), mentally anyway, and he might as well have one for real—she'd felt nothing, nothing at all.

She wasn't interested in anyone! But what really bothered her was that she wasn't making progress. She knew it was going to take a while to get over Roger, but she wanted a little progress.

He used his key when Lizzie was at work to take a look at the cabinets. Jesus, he should never have trusted the guy. The whole time Roger had had to treat him with kid gloves, the artiste, and then the guy had stiffed him! After Roger had looked him straight in the eye and said, "Look, Niles, you've done a great job so far, and I know you're not going to fuck me if I give you the final check before you do the finish work," and then, the check was cashed and that was it—he couldn't even get the goddamn louse on the phone! So here they were, the cabinets, very nice—except, of course, impossible to open without handles.

After he had taken measurements for the hardware, he had an inspiration. Why not clean the fireplaces now, while he was there. Sneak in an extra project when he'd only planned on one—what could be better? It was only one o'clock—if he hurried he could probably get all four done and be gone before Lizzie came home.

He had just about finished the fireplace in the living room when whom should he see through the window walking down Marlboro Street past the house but Jenny Sands. Of all the coincidences, Jenny Sands! Of course, he could only see her from the back, but he was absolutely positive it was Jenny—from the walk, the way she tilted her head a little to the left, even the hair looked as if it were about to turn upwards into a flip for him.

Should he run down the street and catch up with her? What would he say, "How's old Buzz? Divorced yet?" Why was he so sure she would be divorced? Did he really want to see her face? What was she, his age, thirty-four? (No, she was a half-year older, she must be *thirty-five* by now). But of course he was a mess, covered in soot from head to foot. He wouldn't have time to clean himself up if he wanted to catch up with her. He glanced out the window again; she was just getting to the corner. There was still time if he hurried.

But to his surprise he couldn't seem to move. After all those years of carrying her image in his mind, the truth was, he didn't want to see her face. There she was walking down the street, and he hadn't moved an inch.

"You never forget your first love," Jenny had said, but even as he remembered, he knew at last he was beginning to forget.

Besides, he was a mess. He went back up the chimney.

Here Lizzie was, carefully avoiding all guys and somehow or other she was going out on a date with this disc jockey, because she didn't want to be impolite. She'd hired him to do the voice on some radio commercial, and he'd called her up later and asked her if she'd wanted to go out for a bite, and she hadn't known how to say no because she felt it sounded presumptuous of her to assume he was asking her out on a *date*. They were colleagues, after all. What was she supposed to say, "No, I do not want to go out for a bite to eat because I know that all you want is my body and I have given up men and wish that I were dead." Better to go out have a bite and be done with it, treat the whole thing as a couple of colleagues from work, having a beer. Not, of course, that she had ever had a beer with a guy from work (actually, she'd never had a beer in her life) without there having been some kind of sexual tension. All this talk about having guys for friends was never really true; usually at least one of you wanted to sleep with the other. If she couldn't remember exactly what he looked like, she did remember having been very businesslike with him. She dressed carefully in old jeans and a sweatshirt to further her stance.

"Uh-oh," Lulu said, looking out of the upstairs window, "there's someone locking up his white Continental, and he looks pretty dressed up!" There he was in some awful blue suit walking up to the front door.

While she was reluctantly changing into a dress upstairs, she heard through the grate Lulu chatting with James Johnston Jones. Where were they going for dinner? Lulu asked. A nice little restaurant in Hartford, said James Johnston Jones from the depths of his diaphragm. Hartford! She'd *thought* he had said something about Hartford over the phone, but she'd figured she'd misunderstood. When Lizzie came down she offered him a beer for the ride. "Never when I fly," chuckled James Johnston Jones, knowingly, in the voice that launched a thousand records a day. Fly? Fly? Lizzie didn't know what to say. She walked out the door, her heart sinking as James smoothly moved to open the car door for her. She'd heard he'd had three wives already. *Fly?* She *hated* to fly, and within thirty minutes she was up in the skies next to James Johnston Jones in a *two*-seater airplane. She remembered the one time she'd flown in a small plane, a twelve-seater and she'd asked Roger in midflight if small planes were safer or more dangerous than big planes, and he'd said, blithely, safer. When they'd landed she'd said, "You lied?" and he'd nodded. Well, now she was climbing the azure skies with James Johnston Jones. The worst part was that it was beautiful. Why was it the kind of people who owned planes were always like James Johnston Jones?

"Give me your paw," he said. Her paw! Dear Christ in heaven! She gave him her paw, what could she do, she was so petrified she could barely speak. And yet, it was the loveliest sight she had ever seen. And then, like an omen from heaven, they saw the Northern Lights, or so she was told. She hadn't the faintest clue what the Northern Lights were, of course, but evidently they were a big deal. James J.J. was filled with emotion. "Well, boys," he called down to earth, "I got myself a purdy little lady next to me here, and this is a quite a sight. Let's hope for a smooth landing," and down they came to have dinner in the airport restaurant. They'd risked their lives to have dinner in an airport restaurant? She tried to chat merrily away throughout the dinner, but James Johnston Jones kept looking at her morosely with lovesick eyes, sighing, "You're a damned attractive girl." They'd barely met! What's more, nobody had ever liked her because she was a damned attractive girl; she always had to get that personality in there to beef up her appeal, but now here was someone who liked her only for her looks.

She prayed all the way home in the airplane and in the Continental. James Johnston Jones was sighing more and more deeply. Any minute he was going to reach across that crushed velvet interior and touch her. Finally, she burst out, "I'm still in love with my ex-husband!" It was the best thing she could think of.

"Wouldn't it be just my luck," said James sadly. "Here I am next to this damned attractive girl, and she tells me she's still in love with her ex-husband. You know what I was going to do? I was going to take you home to my condo in Lynn and have you for dessert."

Thank God he was turning off toward Marlboro Street; it was only a matter of moments. He walked her dolefully to the door, and she tried to look equally doleful; she didn't want to hurt the guy, but she felt the joy of getting inside her house surging up in her, threatening to betray her. Oh God, *anything* to be rid of him! He was bending toward her, and she let him give her a great big French kiss. She didn't care, she was through the door, and it was closed, locking itself behind her, locking James Johnston Jones out. Rapture flooded through her body. She was alone, without James Johnston Jones, and she had never been so happy! She would never complain about anything again! Never! She sank to her knees in praise of God.

"You're a mama's boy!" Vrisslof had actually shouted out at him as he left. Finally he had roused her to a conclusive statement! He couldn't remember what he had said to prompt it, but finally he had gotten a rise out of the shrink. A mama's boy—what did that mean? Wasn't a mama's boy some wimpy little guy who lived at home with his mother and never got married? He remembered the minister saying how his mother should give him away at the wedding and how excited he'd gotten. So he was a mama's boy. How interesting. Was that why he didn't wear jeans around his mother, was that why he'd never rebelled? Oh, Lizzie would have loved this one. She was always saying he was making her into his mother and striking out against her, because he had never struck out against his mother in his adolescence. But she'd never come up with mama's boy, had she? So he was a mama's boy. There was something he liked about being called this, awful as it sounded—at least it was a diagnosis. So he had been protecting his mother (or something)! Was he mad at his mother for this? A mama's boy was not a particularly comforting name to be called for someone who had always prided himself on his strong opinions—

once he'd been king of the hill, now he was thrilled to be called a mama's boy? Oh, for better or worse, he'd come a long way! And yet, he felt good! It was true! All of a sudden, he felt good.

Later that night, he drove over to Jean Stock's.

Once, in the greatest calm he could muster, he had turned to Jean Stock and said, "I'm thirty-four, and it's fair to say that in thirty-four years of living I have never met a more disagreeable human being than you." That was the day she had yelled at the poor *Boston Globe* reporter who had come in unprepared to do a commentary for the PRV news.

That night, he just walked into her apartment and said, "I'm not going to see you anymore."

"What?" she said, plainly taken aback "Can't we work this out?"

"No, we can't," Roger said and walked away, down her stairs slowly, as if saddened, taking the steps one at a time as if sluggish with dejection when, in fact, of course, he was so glad he'd finally faced up to her, he wanted to jump for joy.

All in all, it had been a good day.

Admittedly, the guy was living with a girl, some quick research had told her, but it was a start. He had just come over from another agency as creative group head, and they had been working together on the "*You* Are Our Interest" campaign for Summit Bank for a couple of months. Lizzie hadn't been in the least bit interested in him, until a week earlier when suddenly his good points had come upon her in an infatuating rush. How had she not known before that true love was sitting behind that desk correcting her body copy on energy improvement loans? Now whenever she showed him copy about putting up storm windows or upgrading the furnace, she got a fuzzy feeling all over. That very day he'd come down to her office and read *Alice in Wonderland* aloud to her for an hour. Oh the glinting of eyes! The whole reason for living was restored. He'd said he was having dinner with some people at the Mexican restaurant a couple of blocks from her house; he might call her later for a drink. Jonathan Coopersmith. Lizzie Coopersmith. An old habit of hers was back.

It didn't even matter if it worked out; it was a start. She had promised God she would be happy and she was happy! Oh, she'd be in love again and remarried at the end of a year or two, she knew it now. She remembered when she was crying her eyes out over Richard Townsend at age twenty and saying my life is over, Rena telling her how lucky she was that she had the ability to fall in love—some people didn't. And yet, she had almost despaired, stuck loving Roger, and Roger (in his way) still loving her, and them not being able—for some mysterious reason well beyond her ken—to be together. Life had seemed suddenly so complex. An entire year had passed since Roger had left and she still felt like she'd lost an arm. But now she realized that though she might miss Roger until the day she died, she could still be happy, and that one day life would be simple again.

The apple blossoms were out on Marlboro Street. So, she noticed, was Hope, lying in her favorite spot on the brick sidewalk at the end of the walk, opening her lower body salaciously to each passerby, hoping for a scratch, then closing herself. How guilty Lizzie had once felt about leaving the dogs cooped up all day, the dogs who always greeted her so rambunctiously when she returned home at night; and then she was sick from work once (a hangover, the only excuse acceptable at Smith, Reilly) and realized that all the dogs *did* all day was sleep, saving up their energy to jump up and down when she came home. Well, maybe not neurotic Leslie, who was always perched on top of the couch in the living room looking intently out the window for Lizzie's return. She had this terrible feeling that Leslie waited in that same spot for her all day.

At any rate, there was Hope, free to roam to the ends of the earth, but lying a couple of feet from the house. Lizzie didn't know whether this was because they were girls or because they were dogs, but Hope and Leslie hungered for home, to be possessed—they could be running free all weekend in Maine, but hear the tinkle of the lifted leash and they would wriggle about you, leaping into the air toward the leash in your hand, begging to be attached.

Someone, probably that damn Niles, had let Hope out, and probably Leslie, too. Where was Leslie? How far away had she run? About six inches, as it happened. There she was, sitting on the front stoop, next to Roger.

"Hi," he said. "I've quit my job to come home and work on the house."

Well, she thought, with a glance at the boxes of laundered shirts, I guess I won't be having ol' Jonathan Coopersmith over tonight. And then she sat down beside Roger and took a swig of beer.